I0553929

THE LEMERONS

The Secret Archives Trilogy: Book 2

VALERIE PURI

Copyright © 2020 Valerie Puri

All rights reserved. No part of this publication may be reproduced, distributed, or transmitted in any form or by any means, including photocopying, recording, or other electronic or mechanical methods, without the prior written permission from the authors, except in the case of brief quotations embodied in critical reviews and certain other noncommercial uses permitted by copyright law.

This book is a work of fiction. Names, characters, places and incidents are products of the author's imagination or are used fictitiously. Any resemblance to actual events, locales, or persons living or dead, is entirely coincidental.

First Edition. Printed in the United States of America.

ISBN-13: 978-1-7324825-2-4

Editing services provided by Brass Rag Press

Cover created by Covers by Christian

Interior formatting by Dark Crown Press

For Jet

ONE

Marlene
_____

S caling the wall was easy. The looming structure surrounded the place Marlene Saunders had called home for the last two hundred years. Any ordinary human would find it difficult to make such a climb. But she was far from ordinary. She was cursed.

Peering down from atop the wall, she gritted her teeth. The swarm of grey-fleshed monsters was a reminder of everything she lost. She hated these things. They ruined the life she once had and everything she tried to rebuild.

Lemerons were brainless creatures. They only sought two things in the world: other lemerons to grow their numbers and to feed on the living. But they never bothered with birds or animals. No. That was not enough to sate their appetite. Only human flesh would do.

Marlene would never fall victim to anyone or anything again. She watched as more lemerons emerged from the forest, gathering at the base of the wall. Their feeble efforts to attack the stones made it seem like they were bored.

Their stench was unbearable. Decay wafted off them like the rotting carcasses that they were. The more there were, the worse the smell. It served them well, as others caught the stench drawing them to the larger group.

Marlene's lip twitched. She wanted to destroy them all right here and right now, but she lacked the strength. They would tear her to shreds before she could kill all of them. She needed help. She needed her husband and his people.

Getting through the hoard would be a challenge. She traded her purple Elder robes for her hardened leather armor for this purpose. Old as it was, her armor was well made. It could withstand a lemeron's claws...for a while.

Marlene squeezed the handle of her sickle. The curved blade saved her life more than once. Her only path forward was through the lemerons. She would cut them down as though she were harvesting the dead instead of a crop.

"Ethan," she whispered to the wind.

She had to reach her son, assuming he was still alive. A knot gripped her stomach. What if her baby never made it? What if Brenden failed to get him to safety?

A few of the closer lemerons heard her. They peered up at her with cloudy yellow eyes. One opened its mouth, revealing blackened teeth. A raspy groan erupted from its throat.

As hardened as she was, the sound still made her shudder.

The other lemerons heard the call of their own and added their cracking voices to the choir of the damned. It was a battle cry. A rally to arms. With frenzied speed, they attacked. They slammed into the wall towering before them. They slashed at each other with razor-sharp nails, destroying one another to get to her.

Peering over the treetops into the distance, Marlene gripped her sickle firmly. She was ready.

She brought the blade to her face, inhaling and exhaling. Without a second thought, she dove from the wall into the sea of monsters.

A crunch of bones broke her fall as she landed on one of the lemerons.

One down, hundreds to go.

All around her, blackened teeth snarled, boney arms lashed out, and claws slashed at her. The monsters pressed forward, overwhelming her stance. She tried to advance, but there were too many. They surrounded her on all sides, forcing her back against the wall. She lost her ground. Soon they would engulf her.

Despite the chill of autumn, sweat dotted her forehead.

Damn. I have to get through. I have to get to Ethan and Brenden.

She was being crushed between the wall behind her and the lemerons.

One roared and lunged at her throat, teeth bared. She fell to her knees to avoid the fatal bite. Her sudden disappearance stunned the lemeron. It couldn't comprehend her changing the rules of the battlefield.

Seizing her chance, she slashed upward with her blade, cutting the monster's chest open. Clumps of brown blood oozed out from the wound, spilling on the dirt by its feet. For any living creature, that would be a death blow. But to a lemeron, it was little more than a mild annoyance.

It looked around, confused. Marlene reached up and grabbed it by the arm, tugging it down. When it stumbled forward, she cut its head off. The lemeron crumpled to the ground in a heap, finally dead.

Two down.

Clambering on top of the fallen lemeron, she stood. She had enough space to swing her sickle. The best way to stop a lemeron was to cut off its head. And so she did.

One after another, she brought down the monsters. Where two fell, one took its place. Her progress was slow, but she was putting distance between herself and the wall.

She cut and slashed through the sea of grey flesh. She was

almost to the edge of the forest. If she made it, she could climb a tree and escape the lemerons.

They seemed to sense her plan. Snarling, they attacked with more vigor. A hot sting ran down her back. Her armor loosened around her waist. More searing burns surged over her back and across her side.

She glanced over her shoulder to see a lemeron behind her. Its hands glistened red with fresh blood. It licked her blood off its fingers with a purple tongue.

Ugh. Marlene groaned with disgust. It had tasted her. It wouldn't stop now until it devoured her.

She had to keep going. Each time she swung her arm to cut down another lemeron, her back flared with pain. She was vulnerable. Her armor failed her.

I have to go on. I have to get to Ethan. I have to tell him everything.

Her head spun. Each effort to push forward, to kill another lemeron, exploded in blazing pain. Her back was soaking wet as if she just emerged from her bath. Only this was not water. It was blood. The lemerons around her could smell it. Their yellow eyes gleamed. Their frenzied attack intensified.

Make it to the tree, just make it to the tree.

Marlene pushed herself. She fought her way forward as darkness closed in around the edges of her vision. When she thought she would lose consciousness, her fingers grasped a branch. "Now climb," she urged herself.

TWO

Jennie
_____

The tolling bell still echoed in Jennie Caraway's mind. Only moments ago, Elder Marlene stood in the bell tower crowning the school, ringing it incessantly. It was a call to the people of the Commune to wake up. Not just from the last dredges of early morning sleep, but to wake up to the treacherous group secretly controlling things in their society. Controlling them.

Marlene exposed Victor Glassman's betrayal for all to hear. He was the other Elder in the Commune; there were always two. Until that morning, Marlene kept silent, letting Victor seize control of the Commune. Anyone who tried to stand in his way or threatened his agenda disappeared.

He never dirtied his own hands. His loyal pawn, Sash, abducted his enemies. No one saw them again... at least not as humans. Victor had them transformed into dociles, mindless creatures who never questioned or talked back. He kept his victims hidden, so people in the Commune were unaware of what really happened to their missing neighbors. Victor would claim they ventured outside the safety of the wall and were killed by lemerons.

The problem was, dociles were too closely related to

lemerons. They were alike in every way, except dociles were passive. They weren't driven by the uncontrollable need for human flesh. Instead, they performed menial tasks to help keep their settlement running. Victor created too many, providing a beacon for lemerons. They were drawn to their kin. Now, the lemerons were gathering at the wall in staggering numbers.

Victor's hidden hoard of dociles would be the Commune's undoing. He was responsible for so much destruction.

Jennie scowled at him from the back of the crowd. Her father and his friend Alan Thompson wrestled Victor from the town square.

"Let me go! I'm ordering you to release me," he cried as he thrashed around. "Marlene's lost her mind. She's lying. You're all fools to believe her."

Jennie scoffed. He was the one who lied to the entire Commune. He and his secret group, the Order, kidnapped her best friend, Belle. All to get to Jennie... and the book. They got her, but never found the journal.

Sash tortured her for information. Her body ached just thinking about it. She was a threat to them, because she knew what they did to those they abducted.

Jennie squeezed Belle's hand, glad they could escape before it was too late.

"Let's get out of here." Jennie had seen and heard enough. There were more important things to do than to listen to Victor spew more of his lies.

"Ready when you are," Ethan said.

Victor drilled into everyone that there were no humans left alive outside the walls. Ethan contradicted that just by existing. But Marlene acknowledged that there were others alive out there. Ethan's people. She would recruit them to her cause to help save the Commune. Ethan had come so close to meeting his mother for the first time, but Marlene left before he could.

His plan was to go after her. She would need his help getting his people to fight for the Commune.

When Ethan departed, Jennie would be with him. She had lost too many people she cared about. She wouldn't lose him too.

They made their way through the packed town square. People bumped and pushed into them from all directions. Everyone was surging toward the steps of the schoolhouse, trying to get a better look at what was going on.

One of their elders left the Commune to seek help from people who shouldn't exist, and the other elder was being deposed.

Jennie couldn't blame them. Under other circumstances, she probably would be eager to get a closer look, as well. But she had seen too much and from far too close.

After finally emerging from the solid mass of people, Jennie could breathe again. Standing in the empty alleyway, she inhaled and instantly regretted it. The putrid stench of the lemerons filled her nostrils. The reek was more prevalent here, away from the crowd. It only intensified the closer they got to the wall... and the lemerons on the other side.

"Ugh, that smell." Travis pinched his nostrils with his fingers.

Ethan nodded. "More are gathering. More will come."

"Thanks for that. I feel so much better." Belle rolled her eyes.

"What will happen now?" Travis asked.

Change always terrified Jennie's little brother. It only got worse after lemerons killed their mother.

Four years ago, the monsters snuck up on them in the woods. Her mother saw them first, screaming for Travis and her to run. They did. But Jennie looked back to make sure her mother was coming too. That's when she saw it all. A lemeron slashed at her mother's face with its claws.

Red gashes opened across her mother's soft cheek sending

blood flowing freely down her face. The lemeron clamped its jaws around her neck, as though it were hungry for her blood.

Jennie shrieked and tripped over a branch on the ground. Afraid she would fall and be the next meal, she looked away. Travis sobbed as he ran in front of her. They made it to the wall and through the gate. Jennie closed the door and did her best to lock it.

She collapsed to the ground, screaming and crying. She couldn't shake the image of what happened. Clutching Travis in her arms, they both trembled. Others nearby heard their cries and came running.

She pushed the thought from her mind. It didn't help to dwell on such dark things from the past.

"We go somewhere safe," she said.

Jennie led the way. There was only one place in the Commune where she truly felt safe: the stables. She was at home with her horses. They were kind, gentle, and loyal. No one ever bothered her or her four-legged friends. It was more of a home to her than the house she shared with her father and brother. The stables were her sanctuary. It was where she felt closest to the mother she lost.

The streets were eerily quiet. Beyond the town square, the Commune felt abandoned. Only the wind swept along the cobblestones where feet would normally tread. The hairs on the back of Jennie's neck stood on end.

A slinking figure darted from behind one building to another. As fast as he or she was, Jennie still spotted them. Whoever it was, they were trying to avoid being seen.

"Someone's sneaking around up there," Jennie warned the others.

"Who do you think it is?" Travis asked.

Belle huffed. "Who else? The Order."

"Not good," Ethan pulled Jennie by the hand down a nearby alley.

This was all so familiar. She fled through these streets with

Belle and Travis once before trying to avoid an unseen foe. That was before everything she ever believed about her home turned out to be a lie. That was before she met Ethan.

Her heart fluttered. It was either from the adrenalin or from the way Ethan squeezed her hand. His firm grip was reassuring. The calluses of his fingers matched her own. He was strong and would do anything to protect her. He already proved that in the brief time she knew him. She would do anything to protect him, too.

The buildings thinned out, and Jennie saw the open fields and the apple orchard ahead. And her beloved stables.

Ethan studied the alleyways behind them. "Whoever that was creeping around, we lost them."

"I'll feel better when we're back inside," Belle said.

Jennie sprinted with Ethan to the safety of the stables. Belle and Travis kept pace behind them.

Jennie had to gather her thoughts, and her belongings, for the trip ahead. She nearly lost her footing as she ran down the hill, her body wanting to move faster than her feet.

She slid open the barn door. After they entered, she shut it, sealing them inside the safety of her stables. It was time to prepare for her trip.

Her stomach fluttered. She had never in her life taken a trip. She would leave the Commune with Ethan. It had been four years since she stepped foot beyond the wall. Back then, she never ventured much past the tree line.

With the lemerons gathering at the wall, she was overcome with nerves. The last time she was on the other side, those monsters attacked then killed her mother. She bit her lip and tasted blood. Sash split it open when he punched her. What little it had healed, she just undid. They weren't safe inside the Commune, and they weren't safe outside its walls.

No matter the danger, she and Ethan would find a way to get help.

THREE

Travis

T ravis looked on as his sister swept through her office, packing her shoulder bag with essentials. As she stuffed a hoof pick in her bag, he wondered what that was for. He didn't think she would really go. Not out there. He couldn't forget what happened. He couldn't forget the screaming.

Four years ago, the monsters killed their mother in the forest. There were only a few of them back then. Now there were dozens, hundreds, maybe even more gathering at the wall. He could see it happening all over again... only this time they would kill his sister.

He closed his eyes, shaking his head, trying to erase the thought from his mind. But it lingered. When he shut his eyes, he could see it more clearly. The half-dead monsters dragging Jennie away into the forest. Her screams ripping through the air, just like their mother's.

"Don't go," he blurted out.

Jennie froze, her hand clutching a roll of bandages. He felt the unasked questions, the stares. Everyone in the compact space seemed to grow until they towered over him.

Belle's tight curls bounced around her face as she shook her head. Ethan cocked an eyebrow at him. No one spoke.

The silence bubbled up and filled the space between them. He wanted to shrink into the corner and pretend he never spoke. But the words were out. He was afraid. Afraid of losing his sister. Afraid of what might happen.

Jennie slid the bandages into her bag. She set it on her desk and stood in front of him. When she placed her hand on his shoulder, he trembled.

He had been so brave when he set out with Ethan to rescue her. That was different, though. Sash took her. He was a monster, but he was human. For some reason, he wasn't as frightening as the lemerons. Those creatures were blood-thirsty monsters and nothing more. There was no hope of reasoning with them. All they knew was death.

"Travis, I have to go."

"But why? What if something happens to you? What if…"

The unasked question hung in the air. The hurt in Jennie's eyes told him she knew what he would ask.

What if the lemerons kill you?

She tightened her grip on his shoulder. "I have to find Ethan's people. We need to see if they can help us get rid of the lemerons. I'll be with him. Together, we'll be fine."

"Why does it have to be you? Why can't he go by himself?"

As soon as the words were out, he felt bad for saying them. He never said the right thing.

Ethan pursed his lips. The way it sounded was like it didn't matter to Travis if Ethan got killed. He could go if he wanted, but Jennie had to stay here so she'd be safe. He bowed his head. He didn't mean for his question to come off like he didn't care about Ethan.

"I never asked your sister to come with me, Travis, but I welcome the support. My mother is out there right now trying to find me and my people so we can help you. We aren't easy to find, so she'll need my help. I - she doesn't know who I am, or that I was even here, so it will be an awkward first meeting."

"And that's where I can help," Jennie added. "Marlene needs to know about Ethan. We lost our mother, let me help Ethan find his."

Travis opened his mouth to respond but thought better of it. If he spoke, he would say no. Knowing Jennie, she might actually stay for her little brother. But if she did, she wouldn't be happy. She would be miserable. She would feel as though she let Ethan down. Travis could tell she cared about Ethan. How could he stand in the way of his sister being happy? How could he stand in the way of Ethan being reunited with his mother?

He couldn't.

Sighing, he relented.

"Okay," was all he said.

There was more that he wanted to say, to warn Jennie of the dangers, to ask her to reconsider. But she knew just as well as he did how dangerous it would be to leave the safety of the wall. And her mind was made up.

She tousled his hair like she always did. It brought a tentative smile to his lips. He wished he could pretend everything was normal, but he couldn't forget. All he could do was hope his worst nightmares wouldn't become a reality with his sister being the lemeron's latest victim.

FOUR

Jennie

Travis hunched his shoulders and stared at his feet. Jennie hated that her decision to leave hurt him, but she had just the thing to cheer him up. It was his birthday, after all, so now was as good a time as any to give him his present.

"Wait here, I'll be right back."

She slipped from her office and made her way through the stables until she came to the stall she was looking for. Taking the bridle off the hook beside the opening, she entered. A midnight black stallion perked up when he saw her. Jennie scratched his chin, and the horse knickered and bobbed his head.

"Come with me. I want you to meet someone," Jennie slipped the bridle over his head.

She walked him down the aisle back toward the others. His hoofs kicking up the soft dirt on the floor. Jennie halted outside of her office and called out.

"Travis, come here. I have your birthday present."

Her little brother emerged from the office. His eyes grew wide when he saw the horse.

"This is Emerald. He's a gentle giant, and as long as you take good care of him, he'll give you lots of affection."

"You mean I can have him?" Travis asked in disbelief.

"Anyone who works in the stables gets to have their own horse. You're thirteen now, and you decided to join me in the stables. It's a wonderful profession to choose. It's one that's very important to our survival. We need to take care of the horses so the farmers can work the fields with them," Jennie grinned and scratched Emerald's chin again. "But Emerald will be exclusively yours. Just like Misty is mine."

Travis gave Jennie a tight hug. The pressure hurt her aching body, but she squeezed him back. When he released her, he stroked Emerald's cheek and forelock. The horse smelled Travis and nuzzled his new owner.

"He likes you," Jennie smiled. "When I'm gone, you'll need to look after all the horses. Make sure they are fed, watered, and their stalls are clean. I know you'll do a good job."

Her little brother's smile faltered when Jennie mentioned she was leaving. Emerald nuzzled him again.

"I won't let you down," he hugged the horse's head.

She nodded, satisfied that he would take care of her duties at the stables.

Belle was next. She didn't have a present for her best friend, but she had a favor to ask. Jennie pulled her to a corner of the office, hoping they were out of Travis's earshot.

"Look after him. Make sure nothing happens to him while I'm away."

Belle nodded knowingly. "Sash won't get anywhere near him."

"Thanks," Jennie glanced over to make sure Travis was still occupied with his present. "There's one more thing. With Marlene gone and Victor out of the picture, the Order might try to make a move. They're power-hungry, and we don't have any elders now. Do what you can to keep them out of power."

"Okay, but what do you expect me to do?" Belle frowned. "We don't even know who's in this Order."

"True," Jennie admitted. Anyone living within the Commune could be part of their secretive group. The unknown enemy. The only people who Jennie was sure were a part of the Order were Victor and Sash. Victor had been removed from power, and Sash was incapacitated. At least for now. Before long, he would come after them again.

Jennie pursed her lips. She was leaving the Commune to face a different danger. But Sash still posed a threat to Belle and Travis, who were staying behind.

"Go to Uncle Albert," Jennie said. "He'll know who you can trust and who should stand in while Marlene is gone."

Her best friend put her hands on her hips. "At this point, I only trust the four people in this barn. But I know Albert's like an uncle to you, so I'll reach out to him."

Belle rushed forward and gripped her in a hug. Jennie winced from pain, but returned the gesture, wrapping her best friend in her arms.

"I'll miss you. Don't be gone too long," Belle pulled away, water glistening in her eyes.

The sight tugged at Jennie's heart. Belle never got emotional.

"I'll be back before you can say 'undesirable.'"

Belle choked out a laugh. "You better, or else I'll have words with Ethan. I wonder, would the Order consider Ethan's people undesirables like us?"

Jennie shrugged. "That depends on if they go against the Order or not. Anyone who isn't part of their secret group is an undesirable. If Ethan's people are anything like him, we'll be bringing back more targets for Sash."

"Then bring as many as you can so we can overpower Sash and his group," Belle said.

Jennie was ready to leave. The longer she delayed, the more tempting it would be to stay. She wasn't looking forward to encountering any lemerons. Glancing around, she noticed Ethan was nowhere to be seen. She stepped out into the central aisle of the stables. She frowned and looked up and down the length of the building. Still no Ethan.

Where did he go? Did he leave without me?

Jennie wouldn't put it past him. He might have left her behind to protect her from danger. If he did, there's no way she could track him down. She didn't know her way through the forest like him. Lemerons would get her for sure before she found Ethan. Was this his way of forcing her to stay? Was this his way of protecting her?

Her heart caught in her throat as she thought about it. Would she even see him again?

Just when she was sure he really left her behind, Ethan climbed down the loft ladder.

Exhaling a sigh of relief, she smiled. When he reached the last two rungs of the ladder, he jumped down, landing in the dirt with a muted thump. He was dressed in his green tunic with his dagger belt cinched around his waist.

Striding up to her, his green eyes were fixed on Jennie. Her stomach fluttered. She was the only one he was focused on. No matter what happened out there, she was sure he would protect her.

"Are you ready to go?" Ethan asked in his smooth voice.

Jennie nodded.

"Don't forget this," Belle said from behind her.

She held out Jennie's bag. She felt her cheeks turn hot. How could she forget her bag she so diligently packed? If she was this careless out there, things could be a lot worse than leaving behind some supplies. She couldn't let herself get so distracted.

"Thanks, Belle."

Jennie gave Travis a hug. "Look after everything for me.

And father. He'll wonder where I've gone. Tell him I'm going for help and this is something I have to do for all of us."

The hint of Travis's Adam's apple bobbed up and down as he swallowed. "He won't understand. He'll be furious."

The past few days turned their world upside down and set the stage for a revolt within the Commune. How much should they tell their father? He didn't know about Ethan. He didn't know the truth about Marlene. He didn't know about what Sash did to them.

"You know what? He's our father. Tell him everything that happened. Everything. We can trust him. Belle, go with Travis. It's better if you both go, so he knows the details of what happened to you, too."

"Don't worry, Jennie," Belle said. "Now get out of here, you're wasting daylight."

She nodded. Her feet took her to the stable door, but part of her heart remained with Travis and Belle. With a trembling hand, she slid the mass of wood open. She squinted against the sunlight as it poured in through the opening.

Jennie wished they could take a pair of horses, but the forest was too thick and unwieldy for such large animals. Tree branches would unseat them as soon as they entered the woods. It was better to go on foot.

The stench of the air outside overpowered the comforting scent of the horses. It smelled like rotting meat. Coughing, she pressed forward, Ethan by her side.

Jennie slid the stable door shut behind her, closing off a part of her life she wondered if she'd ever see again.

FIVE

Sash

___

S ash groaned as he rolled onto his side.

What the hell am I doing on the floor?

He growled as it came back to him. Those damn kids attacked him. He poked at the red-soaked patch on his pants. And they stabbed him.

His head throbbed. His leg stung.

That older kid jabbed the scalpel in his leg. Sash didn't recognize him, but that didn't surprise him. He didn't bother to get to know the undesirables living in the Commune. The Order was the only group of people he cared to know.

He looked around the disheveled room. Medical supplies and trays were strewn across the cold floor. The bright lights reflecting off the stark, white walls made his head pound even more. Those kids escaped. And so did Isaac.

Sash hated Isaac. The vermin wanted Victor's position as head of the Order. Anyone who went against Victor was Sash's enemy.

The rhythmic sound of a broom swishing across the floor caught his attention. He twisted around to see behind him. Goggles was there, sweeping up the mess those undesirables made. The scrawny man's white lab coat hung limply from his shoulders. It was so long, Sash wondered how his legs didn't get tangled up in it. He never noticed it before. Sash usually towered over Goggles. He wasn't accustomed to being on the ground.

Sash gripped the edge of the table and pulled himself to his feet. The effort exacerbated the pain in his leg. He growled through the searing fire that spread from the wound. Standing made his head buzz.

Goggles stopped sweeping and looked at him. The short man went in and out of focus. Sash could see his lips move, but a ringing in his ears drowned him out.

"What is it, Goggles?" Sash growled. He was relieved to hear himself talk. At least he could hear something.

"I said you should take things slowly. Belle injected you with a powerful sedative."

"I'm not one of your damn subjects," Sash grabbed a tray and flung it at the wall.

Goggles backed away with his hands raised. "Of course, of course. I only meant that a normal-sized man would still be unconscious. Even someone of your size may still be feeling the effects."

Sash only grunted. What Goggles thought he should do didn't matter. Sash did what he wanted. He only took orders from Victor and no one else. He leaned against the table where Isaac had been.

"What happened to Isaac?" Sash asked.

"He -- he left."

Sash whirled around, snarling.

"What? I didn't bring him down here for you to let him go. I told you to process him." He approached the tiny man with bared teeth. "Who told you to let him walk out of here?"

Goggles shrank back, holding his broom in front of him as if he were trying to hide behind it. Like that would help. Sash could snap that broom in half like a twig and beat him bloody with it.

"Where did he go?"

Goggles whimpered. "I d-don't know. He didn't t-tell me. He left after all the fighting."

The fighting. That girl Jennie and her friends caused more problems than they realized. The next time he got his hands on them, they would wish they never escaped. Because of them, Isaac was out there somewhere, spreading his lies to the rest of the Order. He had to protect Victor and the Order at any cost.

"How long has it been since Isaac left?" Sash asked.

If it hadn't been too long, he could track him down before he reached the others. Who knew what Isaac planned to tell them.

Before Goggles got a chance to answer, the massive steel door creaked open.

Sash's head whipped around, the action making him dizzy again. His face grew hot with fury. That door was always supposed to be closed and locked from the inside. Goggles neglected one of his primary duties. No one should be able to enter without being admitted.

He was about to berate the fool when he saw who stepped through the door. His mouth fell open. He quickly snapped it shut, grinding his teeth together.

"Isaac Fenske," he growled.

"Jacob Sash," Isaac responded with indifference.

"Don't use that name with me. I hate that name."

"Then 'Sash' it is."

Sash glowered at him. Isaac's face was swollen from the two black eyes, and broken nose Sash gave him. The corner of Sash's mouth twitched with a half-smile as he admired his handiwork.

The moment of satisfaction was short-lived. Something wasn't right here.

"Why would you come back?"

Isaac circled the room. He stopped to examine the drawers

where Goggles kept the bodies of those who failed processing. Continuing on, he ran his finger along the workbench on the opposite wall. Lifting his hand, he rubbed his finger and thumb together.

"I asked you a question," Sash snapped.

Isaac clasped his hands behind his back and approached.

"I take it you haven't heard the news," Isaac said.

"What news? Quit playing games with me."

Isaac closed his swollen eyes and shook his head slowly. "We have been exposed. Victor was overthrown and taken into custody by the undesirables."

Sash staggered backward, pain ripping through his leg. Victor had been his mentor for over twenty years. Without his guidance and instruction, Sash was lost. He felt the color drain from his face.

"What do we do now?"

SIX

Ethan

___

"You said the mass of lemerons is gathering at the north wall by the orchard, right?" Ethan asked.

Jennie nodded. She was biting her split lip again, something she did frequently now.

"Then, we go to the southern part of the wall and exit there."

"But don't we need to go north to find your people?"

"Yes, but it's safer if we go around. It'll cost us more time, but better that than costing our lives."

"I can't argue with that. Then we go south." Jennie turned away from the apple orchard.

They skirted along the edge of the wall. It wasn't worth the risk of cutting through the town and being caught by the Order. Ethan would feel better when he could leave this complicated place behind him.

But now that he had spent time here, and with Jennie, things were different. He wanted nothing more than to return to his home, but he didn't want to leave Jennie. He couldn't ask her to leave her family, friends, and the only life she'd ever known to stay with him.

She might not even like the forest. Sure, she was good at

climbing the ladder to her hayloft, but she might not enjoy living off the ground in the trees. They were still young and had time to figure out their future, whether it be together or apart. He hoped it was together... assuming they lived that long. First, they had to figure out a way to destroy the lemeron hoard.

He took Jennie by the hand. Her fingers were icy, and her palm clammy. Leaving her home was obviously hard on her. Bringing her hand to his lips, he kissed it. He felt her fingers intertwined with his relax.

They rounded the corner of a building, and there it was. The south wall. He didn't have to live here to know which direction they were headed. He was a ranger trained by his father. Navigating unfamiliar landscapes was what he did.

The only time he ever got disoriented was after the lemeron attacked him in the terrible storm. That was the night that changed his life. That was when he found the Commune and what lead him to Jennie.

"Do we climb over?" Ethan asked.

"Goodness, no. That would be too hard."

"What? I did it once before, and that was with a bad arm."

Jennie nudged him with her shoulder. "You don't have to brag," she teased. "Why climb when you can go through?"

"I don't see a door."

"It's hidden behind those bushes."

Jennie pointed to a cluster of thorny shrubs climbing up the wall.

"I'll admit, it's definitely easier than climbing over," Ethan said.

They edged through a narrow gap between two of the bushes. Ethan wriggled like a worm to avoid being jabbed by the thorns. Despite his efforts, he didn't make it through without being snagged and poked a few times. Jennie was petite and didn't seem to be bothered at all by the pesky bushes.

The arched door was nearly as tiny as she was. Metal straps reinforced the planks. The metal had rusted from the weather, leaving orange streaks running down the grey wood.

Jennie fumbled with the rusty metal barring the door shut.

As tall and sturdy as their wall was, it had its weaknesses. This disintegrating piece of wood was one of them.

Finally wriggling the bar loose, she slid it back and pushed the door. She stepped through the narrow crevice. Ethan followed, passing under the massive structure. The wall was at least three times as thick as the door was wide. When they both passed through, Jennie shoved the door shut. A metallic clank followed.

"There," Jennie said. "The old lock still works."

"It locks automatically behind you? How do you get back inside?"

Jennie dusted off her hands. "We used to have people stand guard at the doors. But now that no one ever leaves, we don't need anyone waiting around to open them back up."

"How many of these entrances to the Commune do you have?" Ethan asked.

"Four. One for each direction."

"Let's hope the lemerons don't find the north one."

Jennie shot him a worried look.

Damn it. I should be more careful with my words.

She was risking a lot coming with him. He didn't want to add to her worry about everyone she was leaving behind.

Beyond the wall, this was a strange land for her. He was at home amongst the trees that crept right up to the wall.

Ethan took a deep breath, filling his nostrils with the scent of pine needles and damp underbrush. It smelled like home.

"Oh, that smell," he said. "You can't pick up the lemeron's odor from here."

Jennie's chest rose as she took a deep breath.

"That's good, it means we're safe, at least for now."

"At least for now." Ethan agreed. "We should get moving. We want to put as much distance between us and the wall before it gets dark."

Ethan took the lead, heading southwest to put distance between them and the wall. They would continue in that direction for about a mile, then circle around until they were heading north towards his home.

The leaves on the trees had turned bright yellow, orange, and red. They blended together to create a tapestry of warm colors. When the wind blew, the branches looked like the flickering flames of a fire. The carpet of freshly fallen leaves cushioned their path.

Without debris covering the ground, he could easily spot protruding roots and fallen branches. They were now camouflaged. He was sure-footed and accustomed to walking on uneven terrain, but Jennie wasn't. By taking the lead, he would let her know of any dangers - his toe bumped into a protruding root - like that.

"Watch your step," he said over his shoulder.

He glanced back, making sure Jennie missed the root. Stepping cautiously, she avoided it.

When Ethan focused again on the path in front of him, he froze, his breath catching in his throat. Instinctively, his hand snapped to the dagger on his belt. He ripped it free of its sheath, brandishing it in front of him.

A lone lemeron in tattered rags shambled toward them. Its mouth hung open, exposing blackened teeth.

The lemeron noticed their presence and released a crackly growl. The sound sent an icy chill through Ethan's entire body.

Jennie gasped. He was more afraid for her than he was for himself. He had to protect her, no matter the cost.

"Stay behind me. No matter what, don't let it bite you."

SEVEN

Jennie

J ennie fished in her bag for something, anything, that she could use as a weapon. Her fingers wrapped around a little metal rod with a bent tip. A hoof pick.

The lemeron's crackling shriek sent shivers through her body. The creature advanced with startling speed. It stumbled over the roots snaking across the forest floor. For a shambling corpse, it was agile.

Its yellow eyes locked on to her. That rabid stare made her shudder. The last time she laid eyes upon a lemeron was when a few of them killed her mother. That was something she never wanted to remember.

Now this one was out to kill her, too.

Trembling, she brandished the hoof pick in front of her. The lemeron reached out and slashed the air as it charged.

Her fingers turned to pudding. The metal pick fell to the ground with a soft thump. She staggered back, her heel catching on a root. She fell to the ground, her body cracking against the rock-laden earth. Pain seared through her, but fear drowned out the sensation.

She scrambled away, kicking leaves up with the effort.

The lemeron craned its head in a stiff circle and leapt at her with bared teeth.

Jennie screamed. She threw her arms up to cover her head, just as her mother had done.

"I told you to stay behind me!"

Ethan ran into the lemeron, smashing into its side while it was still airborne. The creature's arms flailed as it crashed into a nearby tree. Ethan rushed it before it could recover. With his knife, he sliced through its neck. Jennie cringed at the sound of metal scraping against bone. She looked away as Ethan continued to saw through the lemeron's neck.

It screeched again, then let out a gurgling sound. She heard two distinct thuds on the leaf-covered dirt.

Looking back over at the tree, Jennie saw the lemeron's body lying motionless on the ground, its head a few feet away.

Ethan's back was to her. His shoulders rose and fell rapidly as he panted from the effort of the attack. He turned to face her.

Jennie's hands shot to her mouth.

He was covered in the creature's brown blood. If she didn't know any better, she would have thought he was covered in mud. But she knew better. He was dripping wet with lemeron gore. He wiped his knife clean on his sleeve and sheathed it in his belt.

His nose scrunched in disgust as he examined his hands. He wiped them on his pants.

"Why didn't you stay behind me?"

The harshness in his voice startled Jennie. His green eyes bored into her.

"I..." her voice trailed off.

She felt sick to her stomach. She faltered. She almost died... or worse. She couldn't even protect herself.

Jennie didn't know what to say. It all happened so fast.

After everything she'd been through and how she always fought to survive, she froze. Everything she was melted away until all that was left was fear. The lemeron almost killed her. If Ethan hadn't been with her...

Her hands shook. She looked at her trembling fingers, the fingers that betrayed her. When it mattered most, she dropped the only thing she had that could be called a weapon.

"Hey, it's all right." Ethan's voice softened.

He crouched beside her. His emerald eyes filled with concern.

"I'm sorry if I came off too harsh. I was just worried. If anything happens to you out here..." He shook his head. "I could never forgive myself. I'm angry with myself, not you. I almost failed you."

Jennie furrowed her brow.

"What do you mean?"

"I swore I would protect you and that lemeron nearly got you. I almost failed."

Jennie looked back at her hands. They were still shaking. She barely made it a hundred feet from the wall, and at the first real danger, she became a coward.

"No, you saved me. I failed myself," she choked out.

Ethan took her hands in his. His skin was sticky with the lemeron's clumpy blood.

He helped her up to her feet. She brushed the dead leaves off her pants as she tried to steady her nerves.

You can do this. Don't give in to the fear.

Ethan brushed a strand of hair from her face. "You don't have to come with me, you can still go back inside your wall where it's safe."

"It's not safe for me anywhere. Better I go with you than stay behind for Sash to attack me again."

"Then stay close. We need to move faster than originally

planned. The last thing we want is to run into more of those." He gestured with his thumb to the dead lemeron.

He trotted into the woods. Jennie took a deep breath.

You can do this.

She jogged after Ethan, going deeper into the woods than she ever had before.

EIGHT

Marlene

The lemerons were fast, but she was faster. Marlene escaped the hoard at the wall, but some gave chase. Her back stung from the deep scratches their claws left. Her skin would heal, and her leather armor could be mended, but it would never be as strong again.

The shredded leather hung like ribbons trailing behind her as she leapt from branch to branch. Lemerons couldn't climb, so she was safe as long as she remained in the tree canopy. Beneath her, the grey creatures followed like a rushing river snaking along the ground.

She had to lose them. If they continued their pursuit, she risked leading them right to the other's settlement, Arborville. To her son. She gave him up to keep him safe. She would be damned if she knowingly brought more lemerons to him.

With the growing number of monsters approaching the Commune, many had to pass right by Arborville. The lemerons may have already attacked them. For all she knew, he could be dead already.

Marlene leapt to another branch. The impact of her landing causing it to shudder. It cracked beneath her feet. She tried to grab hold of another limb to brace herself, but the one she stood on gave way. It was falling, and she with it. Plummeting to the ground would mean certain death. The lemerons swarmed beneath her, hungry for her flesh.

For nearly two hundred years, she had evaded them. This was not the end. Not for her. Not today. She jumped from the falling limb. Reaching out, she grabbed at the tree. Her hands gripped the stub of the broken branch. Her body slammed into the trunk of the tree, knocking the breath out of her. Her back stung as she strained to hang on.

The tree limb crashed to the ground, crushing a lemeron beneath it.

Good. One less to worry about.

Hanging with her hands above her head was excruciating. The skin on her back stretched, pulling the fresh gashes open. She cringed and pulled herself up. Pain surged across her skin as the cuts threatened to tear further.

She kicked her foot out, trying to find purchase. Finally, her toe caught hold of a low branch. Using it as leverage to push herself up, she climbed the trunk of the tree like a four-legged spider. Each movement sent more pain shooting through her back.

It was too much. She needed to rest or she wouldn't heal. Her injuries would only get worse. Exhaling, she eased herself onto a sturdy branch. She gingerly reclined against the tree. She needed rest.

She slowed her breathing. Marlene's heart beat in time with her throbbing pain. Low moans from the lemerons rose from the ground. She was high enough now that they would lose her scent. They were growing placid. Soon they would disperse, seeking others of their kind.

Is it wrong to wish for them to go to the Commune and leave me alone?

As an Elder, it was Marlene's job to lead and protect her people. She gave up everything for the sake of the Commune.

Her self-serving thoughts were justified. For once, she would do something for herself. She would put herself first and find her son. Only then would she help the others.

She closed her eyes, letting the low groans of the lemerons lull her to sleep.

When she opened her eyes again, she felt like a new person. Stretching out her arms, she shrugged the sleep from her shoulders like a loose cloak. Moving didn't hurt any longer. It felt good. The new patches of skin on her back itched. She enjoyed the scratch as she rubbed her back against the tree trunk.

Completely healed and rested, she was ready to continue her journey. The lemerons were gone. Having grown idle and forgetting their prey, they moved on. The pull of the hoard at the wall proved too strong for them. They longed for it. It was like being pulled into a state of pure ecstasy.

Marlene felt it, too. It was always there, a tuneless song humming in the back of her head. Now that she left the confines of the Commune, it had grown louder. She wanted to be a part of it, but the source would kill her.

The hum came from each lemeron. If she sought it out, as they did, they would tear her apart limb from limb. To them, she was another human to devour. They lacked the capacity to understand how much like them she really was.

So, she pushed all thoughts of the song from her mind. It was just something that was there. Like the wind rustling the leaves, or the birds chirping among the trees. The farther she got, the quieter the song would become. The pull on her would weaken.

Jumping from the tree, she landed on the ground in a crouching position. Without pausing, she broke into a run. It was much faster traveling on the ground. It took too long leaping from branch to branch. At this rate, she would reach Arborville by the next day.

NINE

Sash

"You meant nothing to Victor. You were just a tool he used to get the job done," Isaac leaned against the wall, keeping one of the metal tables between him and Sash.

"No, you're wrong," Sash gripped his head.

His skull was still pounding from whatever the curly-haired girl injected him with. Isaac's lies didn't help.

"Victor was my mentor. He always looked after me. He supported me more than anyone."

"And he used you," Isaac stated flatly.

"No!" Sash grabbed the metal table between them and heaved, toppling it over. It crashed against the floor.

Goggles jumped with a start and slunk out of the room like the weakling he was. He went into his office and shut the door. It didn't matter. Sash would deal with him later.

He was sick of the deceit, the lies. Isaac was out to seize control of the Order, and to do that he needed Victor out of the way. Sash wouldn't let him get away with it.

"I didn't have to come back here, but I did. I left of my own free will and I came back of my own free will. You know what's at stake here, Sash. This is bigger than you and me."

He looked into Isaac's brown eyes, framed with dark bruises.

"Victor got careless. He went after the wrong people. Because of that, he exposed us all. Everyone knows about the Order now. Marlene made sure of that when she outed Victor to the entire population of the Commune. Those of us present tried to cast doubt over her claims, but too many undesirables spoke up to support her."

"What?" Sash was stunned. "Marlene did that? She's never spoken out against Victor. She's not one of us, but why would she go against her fellow elder?"

Isaac smiled. "Now you're using your head, Sash. She has a motive that is unclear to us. Given time, we'll expose what it is and destroy it… along with her."

It was Sash's turn to smile. Elder or not, if Marlene turned out to be an undesirable, he would enjoy bagging her.

"I can see that pleases you. Good. But you should know, she's out of our reach right now. She fled beyond the wall, claiming there are others out there who can help us."

Sash furrowed his brow. "There's no one left alive out there."

Isaac cleared his throat. "Yes, that is what we all understand as the truth. And what we must continue to teach."

Sash nodded slowly. *Why would she spread such lies? If there were people living outside the wall, why would they even be willing to help her?*

"Wait. You said she went to find help? Help with what?"

"You're smarter than Victor gives you credit for, Sash."

Sash opened his mouth to comment, then frowned. That sounded like a compliment, but at the same time, Isaac made it seem like Victor didn't think much of him.

"Marlene claims there are many lemerons gathering at the wall," Isaac went on. "She blames Victor for it because he's been creating dociles. The lemerons are drawn to each other, and also to the dociles we have here. These are her claims. It's all baseless. There's no evidence that lemerons are attracted to each other like a magnet to metal."

These thoughts made the pounding in Sash's head intensify. He couldn't think clearly.

"What does this have to do with Victor using me?" Sash grumbled, losing his patience.

"Victor deviated from the original plan years ago. You were instrumental in making that possible for him. No one would dare touch him so long as you were around to protect him and obey his every command."

"You make me sound like a docile. I'm capable of doing more than one thing." Sash snarled through gritted teeth.

"Evidently so, but Victor didn't think that. He only saw what your physical strength could do for him. He overlooked your most valuable asset: your mind."

Victor *had* asked for his input on important matters before… hadn't he? The more Sash thought about it, the less he thought it was true. Did Victor really only use him like a docile?

"Aside from Victor, we all saw your value. When you weren't around, I made sure the others in the Order knew of your unwavering loyalty and dedication to our cause. Without you, Victor wouldn't have amounted to anything. You were what made it all possible for him."

The corner of Sash's mouth curved upward in a half-smile. It felt good to be recognized for his work.

"But, Sash, understand that what you made possible is what may lead to our downfall."

His smile fell. "What do you mean?"

"Victor became a liability. If Marlene hadn't made his actions known, causing the people of the Commune to depose him, we would have silently removed him. It's a shame it all had to happen so publicly."

Isaac shook his head as if remorseful.

"It all started when Victor had James Townsend

processed. That one act threw everything we worked so hard for into jeopardy. After that, he became careless. Too many people were disappearing and too quickly. Eventually, people would become suspicious. And they did, as you well know."

"What of it?" Sash asked. *Where is he going with all of this?*

"You never questioned a single order Victor gave. He had you remove so many citizens of the Commune, even some school children became aware something was wrong," Isaac sighed. "I'm sorry Victor took advantage of you like that. He exploited you and your skills. Now he's gone, and the Order needs you more than ever. I assure you of this: we will never take advantage of you like Victor did. You are a brother of the Order, it's time you were treated like one."

There were so many times where Victor barked commands at Sash. He did things no one else would, all in the name of loyalty to his mentor. He kidnapped, tortured, and killed. All for what? So Victor could advance his own agenda? They were supposed to achieve great things *together*. They were supposed to execute the plan that nearly took two decades to prepare for.

Sash thought back to the night when he attacked Isaac. It had been at Victor's request. He looked at his hands. The same hands he reddened with the blood of his brother of the Order.

"You never betrayed the Order. Victor told me himself, only after I attacked you. He staged the night he was late, knowing you would take charge. He used me to remove you. You weren't trying to overpower him like he claimed. You were trying to see the plan through," Sash sank down to the floor. "What have I done?"

"What you thought was right," Isaac knelt down beside him, placing a hand on his shoulder. "Now work with me to take back the Commune, my brother. Together, we can succeed where Victor failed."

TEN

Travis

"**W**hat?" Jack Caraway, Travis's father roared.

He paced the tiny kitchen, his voice filling the cramped space.

Travis left out the part about Belle and Jennie being kidnapped. He and Belle agreed it would be best to not mention it to his father. He was sure his father might put his fist through the wall if he found out.

"You and Jennie disappear for days on end, and now you tell me she left the Commune with some strange boy?" Jack pointed an accusing finger at Travis, who shrank in his chair. "What in the hell is she thinking? What are *you* thinking? There's no such thing as a stranger. We are the only people left in the world. And what about the lemerons in the forest? Have you forgotten what happened to your mother? How could you let Jennie leave? What if something happens to her?"

"I will never forget what happened to mother. For four years, I've relived how she was killed every night in my nightmares." Travis shuddered.

He should have known better than to let Jennie go with

41

Ethan. He should have done more to stop her. His father was right; it was too dangerous out there.

"If anything happens to her, so help me," Jack raised his hands in the air, his frustration apparent.

"Mr. Caraway," Belle cut in. "Everything Jennie has done, and is still doing, is all to save the Commune."

"Save the Commune?" His father scoffed. "It doesn't need saving. Victor's done for, and the wall will stand for hundreds of years. The lemerons are no threat to us. We're safe here."

Belle exchanged a doubtful look with Travis. "I'm not so sure about that," she said.

"You're the expert now?" Jack asked. "Playing with solar panels doesn't make you a mason."

Belle's nose flared.

This was not going well. Travis bit his tongue, afraid anything he said right now would make this argument even worse.

"And being a blacksmith doesn't qualify you either," she retorted.

His father squared his shoulders and took a step towards Belle. He narrowed his eyes at her.

"You kids think you have it all figured out, don't you? I've seen more things than you can imagine. You have no idea about what really happens in this place."

Belle folded her arms defiantly. "Oh, you mean like disappearances being covered up as lemeron attacks so the Order can create more dociles? Or do you mean being kidnapped and tortured for information by a secret organization?"

His father opened his mouth to speak but faltered. "What do you mean kidnapped and tortured?"

"Just because Victor was exposed doesn't mean the threat is gone. Sash is still out there and he's dangerous. If it weren't for Travis and Ethan, you would never have seen either of us again. They rescued us from Sash."

His father's mustache twitched. Red boiled up his neck into his face.

He rounded on Travis. "Why didn't you tell me any of this?"

Travis gripped the arms of his chair. Now Belle had really done it. The secret was out. He would be in so much trouble and his father would never let him out of his sight again.

Swallowing the frog in his throat, he mustered the courage to speak up.

Belle cut in before he could answer. He exhaled in relief, slouching back in his chair.

"What's the point? What's done is done. Without Victor ordering Sash around, we can take him down."

His father shook his head. "That's where you're wrong. With no one directing him, that bald-headed freak is more dangerous than ever."

Travis scrunched his face and his stomach lurched. "How would you know something like that?"

"You stepped into the middle of a silent war that's been going on for decades. You may not have realized it, but you've felt the effects."

His father sat down at the table across from him. Travis's face paled. It felt like his heart was being crushed. He glanced over at Belle, leaning against the kitchen sink.

"That teacher, Mrs. Townsend?" Jack continued. "She was too ambitious. We warned her not to be so direct, but she wouldn't listen. Her need to expose the Order blinded her. She thought it would help her get her husband back, but she was wrong." He slammed his fist on the table. "And now, because of her carelessness, you got pulled into this mess."

Belle uncrossed her arms and stepped forward, her curls bouncing with the sudden movement. "Whose side are you on?"

Dang. I knew Belle was fiery, but she's taking fearless to a whole new level.

His father set his jaw, studying Belle.

Finally, he answered. "There are some of us in the Commune who refuse to stand by while we are purged. I will not fall victim to Victor's lot. I will not let my children fall into their hands. If you're as smart as you think you are, you won't get involved. Walk away while you still can."

"It's too late for that. I've already been kidnapped, tortured, and added to the list of future dociles. Tell me how I can walk away from that and be safe."

Jack shifted in his chair.

"Father," Travis mustered his courage to speak. He had to know for certain. "Are you with the Order?"

His father grimaced.

"Have I given you reason to think so?"

Travis rubbed his sweaty palms on his pants. "You're not answering the question. I need to hear you say it. Are you with the Order?"

"No. I align with another group entirely. It's not safe for me, or you, if I talk about it."

Travis felt the color return to his face. The fist gripping his heart relaxed.

"Then we know who you're with," Belle nodded approvingly. "The Truth Seekers."

"Belle, what are you doing?" Travis hissed. "What if my father isn't with them? We shouldn't be running around blabbing about the Truth Seekers."

Belle pursed her lips, unconcerned.

"He said he's not with the Order," she shrugged.

He didn't know who he could trust. There were two Truth Seekers that he knew of, Uncle Albert and Marlene. Marlene was gone, so that left Albert.

"Father, I want to believe you, but why are you being so secretive?"

Jack raised an eyebrow in response.

Travis stood from his chair, the force smacking it into the wall. He gripped his hair and paced the tiny kitchen

"I don't know what to think anymore. Too much has happened in the last few days. Victor had Sash kidnap Mrs. Townsend. Then he got Belle and my sister who were tortured. There are still people alive outside of the Commune." He tugged at his hair, wanting to rip it out in frustration. "And to top it all off, a bunch of lemerons are piling up at the wall just waiting to get inside and kill us all. How is this even normal?"

The cracked walls of the kitchen were closing in around him. The cramped space was suffocating.

"I need to get out of here. I need fresh air *and* some answers."

He opened the back door leading outside. Before slamming it shut behind him, he shouted, "this is the worst birthday ever!"

ELEVEN

Belle
_____

"Travis, wait up," Belle jogged after him outside.

He was shorter than her, but he was quick. It was probably from all the practice he got rushing to school. Travis was always running late, so he always ended up running.

He halted and turned around, his face red as a strawberry.

"Why'd you have to tell my father about you and Jennie being kidnapped? We agreed not to tell him."

"Look, Travis, I lost my cool, okay? In the moment, it was the only way I could think to make him understand how much we've been through. None of us are safe as long as the Order's still in power. You know that. I know that. Hell, even Ethan knows that, and he's not even from here."

"Because of you, I'm doubting my father. I wish he wasn't so secretive about this." He lowered his voice. "And then you had to mention the Truth Seekers to him. What if he really is with the Order? What then? We aren't safe anywhere in this place." Travis turned his back on her. "I wish you never said anything to him."

Belle's stomach plummeted.

"You have a point…. We don't know who we can turn to. But do you really think your father is working with *Sash*?"

She laughed at the possibility.

Travis's face grew redder as his nostrils flared. "I don't see what's funny about that. You made us walk right into this mess because you 'lost your cool.' Your attitude could get us killed!"

My parents always said my temper would get me into trouble.

They were right. To her, everything in the world was binary, Just like the circuit boards at the solar farm. On and off, black and white, right and wrong. She lost her temper more than once at the solar farm.

One of her coworkers habitually used the wrong wire. Sure, it worked, but only for a little while. The gauge was too small and couldn't handle the electricity load for long. It would fry a capacitor, and then they would have to redo the entire thing. She hated fixing other people's lazy mistakes, and she made it known.

Carelessness was just another way of muddying the waters. Her coworkers called her a perfectionist. They meant it as a slight, but she wore it like a badge of honor.

"Your father insulted me." She crossed her arms. "He basically called me a naive little child. I know more of the darkness in this place than he could imagine. Letting him know it seemed like the right thing to do in the moment."

"And how did it help us?"

"Well," Belle said.

"It didn't." Travis cut her off. "Find another way to help out, because whatever you think you're doing isn't working."

Her mind drifted back to the barn loft. She stashed the bin full of incriminating files she stole there. They were Alex Richardson's files detailing the deaths and so-called successes of his subjects.

He vanished a few years ago, and no one had seen him since. Belle had, though. He now went by the name Goggles and worked day and night creating more dociles. He wanted to turn her into a docile.

"I can't just wait for them to take me again and turn me into some gray skinned, bald-headed, yellow-eyed monster."

Belle shuddered just thinking about it. Her teacher Mrs. Townsend was undergoing that very process. Goggles was turning her into a docile.

She escaped a nightmare. If Travis hadn't come with Ethan, both she and Jennie would be the next mindless shells working behind the blue glass in the kitchens. Mr. Caraway had to know. It was the right thing to do. Wasn't it?

"I'm sorry, but I had to tell your father what happened to us."

Travis shook his head. "Maybe, but that wasn't the way to do it. I don't know. I just need to figure some stuff out." He looked over his shoulder at her. "Do you know who we can trust?"

"There are very few people I can trust right now. And two of them left the Commune."

He raised his eyebrows. "Only two? You can't trust Marlene?"

"The fact that out of the three people we know who left, Marlene is the one you single out as untrustworthy says a lot about her. I trust Jennie, Ethan, and you. Who else is there?"

"Uncle Albert," Travis walked away from her. "And that's who I'm going to see."

"He'll have some answers. I'll come with you."

"No, you won't."

The force behind Travis's command caught her off guard.

"You've already caused enough trouble in my house. I need to do this alone."

Travis disappeared between two houses.

"Great," Belle groaned. Before Jennie left, she made Belle swear to two things: look after Travis and protect the balance of the Commune. She already failed at the first one. The way things were going, it wasn't looking good for the second either.

TWELVE

Sash

Sash had a new purpose. Never again would he be used to fulfill someone else's agenda. From that point on, he would only serve the Order. The true Order. Not the distorted illusion Victor had fed him for years.

"You must remain hidden for some time while we regroup," Isaac instructed. "Too many undesirables know who you are and your affiliation with Victor. Give it a couple weeks. Everyone will forget, and you'll be like a new person to them."

"The undesirables are ignorant," Sash scoffed. "People fear me when I pass by. They'll never forget me."

He puffed out his chest, proud of the status he had achieved.

"You give them too much credit, Sash. With the gathering lemerons distracting them, they will forget Victor and what you've done in his name within a fortnight," Isaac stroked his chin.

Sash recalled how he was allowed in Victor's dwelling in the Sanctuary tower, but he was never treated as an equal and rarely allowed to sit. He was worth more than just being a pawn in Victor's game of chess.

Now the board was cleared, and a new game was set. This time, Isaac would win with Sash at his side.

"What do you need me to do? What's my next move?"

"I need you to stay down here with Goggles. Repair the damage done by those who escaped," Isaac gestured to the chaotic state of the room.

Medical carts were upended, canisters, and vials of liquid lay smashed on the ground. It was a ghastly state for the space Goggles always kept so pristine.

Sash nodded. "I'll do it. What else?"

"I need you to protect him. The escapees know about this place. They may come back with others, looking to expose our innermost workings to the rest of the Commune. Until now, it's been only words and Victor's foolish outburst," Isaac crossed his arms. "No solid evidence of our plan has surfaced. Yet. I need you to make sure it stays that way."

A sneer spread across Sash's face. Anyone who dared enter through the massive door with the rusty lock would face his wrath. He pictured the curly-haired girl slipping inside. She would pay for injecting him with that needle. He would enjoy strapping her down and submitting her to countless tortures. She would beg for death. He would never give it to her. No. She would live on as his brainless servant.

Sash would enjoy the way her skin sagged off her bones as the transformation took over. He'd seen it enough times to know when the final spark of intelligence was suppressed, leaving nothing left of his victim but a docile. Another mindless creature to do the jobs no one else wanted.

His sneer widened to a grin. Oh, how she would pay for attacking him. And the rest of her band, too. The other girl and the two boys. He wished they would come pay him a visit in Goggles's lab.

"I look forward to it," he said, licking his thin lips.

Isaac clapped him on the back. Pain throbbed against

Sash's skull with the impact. He tensed, his attack reflex in full swing.

"Sash the dependable. I knew I could trust you."

He puffed out his chest again. Finally, he had a purpose again. For years, he had to fight to earn Victor's approval. Never quite being an equal, but always used to advance the agenda. Now, Isaac was offering him the opportunity to truly be an equal part in driving the Order's initiative.

The sinking feeling in his stomach was fading, just as the throbbing in his head eased.

He glanced over at Goggles, who was back to sweeping the floor. Something about the slow, methodical way he brushed the broom across the floor reminded Sash of a docile. The steady rhythm was just how one of the creatures would do it. He was working as if in a trance, his eyes hidden behind his lenses.

This scrawny man was the key to the Order's success. He was the very picture of helplessness. Sash despised weak people, and Goggles definitely couldn't fend for himself. At the slightest jab, he toppled over when the intruders entered.

That's why Isaac trusts me to protect him. If anything happens to him, we fail.

"I need to return to the surface now," Isaac said, interrupting Sash's musings. "With Victor removed and Marlene gone, there's unrest among the Commune. It's the perfect time to plant one of our own in a position of power."

Sash grinned. "You're shaping up to be more cunning than I gave you credit for. Those undesirables are in for a surprise when they realize they lost. The Order is everywhere and too powerful to fail. You will carry on where Victor couldn't."

Isaac placed a firm hand on Sash's shoulder. "Protect Goggles. Protect our secrets. The silent war continues."

THIRTEEN

Ethan

_____

After three days in the forest, Ethan was ready for their journey to be over. Not for him, but for Jennie's sake.

One night when she peeled off her boots and socks to rest her feet, he noticed how red and swollen her blisters were.

"Are those new boots?" Ethan asked. "New boots always rub my feet raw."

"No, but they're chafing in places I'm not used to. It's the rough terrain. It's harder than walking on the smooth ground back at the Commune."

Ethan sat down near her and took her foot in his hands. He used his thumbs to massage the bottom, careful not to touch the blisters on the sides.

Her shoulders slouched as she leaned back against a tree trunk. "That feels nice." She closed her eyes.

"We'll reach Arborville soon. Then we can get into the safety of the trees."

"I still can't picture houses built off the ground," Jennie said. "They may be safe from lemerons, but what about bears? They can climb. After running into that one earlier, I am not in a hurry to meet another."

Ethan smiled. "Just be glad it was a bear and not another lemeron."

"Believe me, I am," Jennie said.

"At least the bear didn't bother us and moved on. To answer your question, no. Bears don't come around our homes."

Ethan wished he could have more moments like that. Sitting with Jennie, talking, and making her feel relaxed and safe. Instead, they were still trekking through the forest. Until they reached his home, they were still in danger. Lemerons could be over any hill or behind any tree.

After the first attack, Ethan was cautious. He listened for the woods to tell him the way. When the birds sang, it was safe. When the forest grew quiet, it meant danger was near. The birds and animals could sense when the lemerons grew close, and so they fled. Their absence was a prelude to danger. Ethan lead Jennie away from the potential threat whenever the forest grew silent.

At night, they were stationary. After the hours of rigorous travel, they had to get their rest. Each night, Ethan and Jennie would take turns sleeping while the other kept watch. He took the first watch, letting Jennie get her rest.

On the first evening, he watched her slow and steady breathing as she slept. She was so peaceful, despite all the surrounding danger. When it was her turn to be lookout, he considered letting her sleep. But he needed to rest if he was to lead them in the morning.

Sleep evaded him. In his mind, every twig snapping or leaf rustling was an approaching lemeron. Just when his eyes closed and sleep would overcome him, he would hear a noise. Snapping awake, he would grip his dagger. Careful not to alarm Jennie, he would give the excuse of having to use the bathroom, then scout around their camp. To his relief, he never found a lemeron.

It happened all three nights since they had left. He barely

slept, and when he did, it was only for a few minutes at a time. He couldn't go on like this. Exhaustion would overtake him. He was just as relieved as Jennie to approach Arborville.

The first thing he wanted to do when he got home was to take off his boots and sleep in his wool stuffed bed. The mere thought of the soft mat was enough to make him yawn. His hand fell to the hilt of his dagger. He had to stay alert.

The sound of water trickling over rocks came from the trees up ahead.

"Hear that?" he asked.

Jennie paused before answering. "It sounds like a stream."

"It means we're close."

Jennie sighed audibly. "Thank goodness. I don't know how much more my feet can take. It feels like I walked a mile across hot cinders."

He stepped onto a fallen tree. It spanned the width of the creek, creating a bridge over the flowing water below. Reaching down, he offered his hand to Jennie. Her skin was soft as bird feathers, and a little scratchy like them too.

But her fingers were stiff as ice. The night's chill was setting in. If he had gloves on him, he would've offered them to her without hesitation. But all he had were the clothes he wore and his dagger.

"Just another mile," Ethan reassured her.

She flicked a smile at him. As weary as she was, she kept going. He admired that about her. On the other side of the tree bridge, she hopped down. She landed gracefully but whimpered with the impact. He knew that had to hurt her feet.

As they climbed the sloping hill, the ground transitioned from untamed wild to a well-traveled path. Ethan caught a whiff of meat cooking. Venison. His stomach growled loudly. He flexed his abs, trying to quiet the rumblings.

Over the last three days, they had eaten the provisions Jennie brought from the Commune. While the apples, dry bread, and cured meats kept them going, he craved a proper stew. His empty stomach churned with hunger.

"Do you want something to eat?" Jennie reached her hand into her bag. She took out an apple and offered it to him.

More than anything, he wanted a piping hot bowl of stew to warm him from the inside out. But not wanting to offend Jennie, he took the apple.

"Thanks," he bit into the fruit. It was crisp and sweet. He wanted to save as much room as he could for a hearty meal, but his stomach thanked him for the apple. He finished and tossed the core into the woods. One of the forest critters would find it and enjoy a delicious snack.

"Aren't you hungry?" Ethan asked.

She didn't have an apple along with him. Come to think of it, she hadn't eaten much since they left the Commune.

"That was the last of our food," she said.

The apple turned sour in Ethan's stomach. He assumed she had an ample supply of apples and dried meats in her bag. He felt awful eating the last of their provisions.

"You should have told me. I would have gladly let you have the last apple."

"It's all right. You said we'd be there soon, anyway. I'll eat something when we get there. Besides, you need to keep up your strength in case another lemeron attacks us."

Ethan stopped at the familiar clearing in the forest. He turned and took Jennie's hands in his.

"You know I would sacrifice anything for you. Even my last meal."

Her soft lips turned up at the corners. The cut on her lip was healing. So was the gash in her cheek. He couldn't resist that smile. Ethan kissed her. She leaned into him. He wrapped his arms around her, pulling her closer.

The apple danced in his stomach. His friend, Tulsi, always called the sensation butterflies. She said she always got butterflies in her stomach when she was nervous or excited.

Ethan was definitely not nervous. Being with Jennie thrilled him. He had never known anyone as brave or kind as her. He never wanted to let her go.

A gust of frigid wind rushed through the trees. Jennie shivered in his arms. As much as he wanted to continue embracing her, he didn't want her to freeze. Ethan cupped her cut cheek in his hand and broke off the kiss. She nuzzled against his palm.

I would do anything for you.

"Come on, let's get you inside so you can warm up." He took her by the hand and lead her past the clearing. "We're almost there."

It would be nice introducing her to his friends. And he got to bring her home to meet his father. There were those butterflies again. Ethan wondered what he would think of Jennie. He hoped his father would approve of her.

Of course he would. What's not to approve of? He reassured himself.

A quail called from the trees above. Ethan smiled. Quails lived on the ground, not in the trees, but it was the call of home. His people would whistle a quail call when they saw someone coming or going. It was their way of acknowledging the traveler - usually a hunter or ranger - was safe. From the trees, the scouts could scan the forest for lemeron threats.

The quail whistle rang out again. A rope ladder dropped from a tree beside him.

"Welcome to my home," Ethan said. "Welcome to Arborville."

FOURTEEN

Jennie

"I don't see any buildings," Jennie said, "only trees."

Ethan chuckled. "You're so used to keeping your eyes on the ground. Look up."

She craned her head back and gasped.

Above them, houses were built around the tree trunks, their floors supported by the tree's branches. Suspension bridges made of rope and wood planks connected the houses. It was like a giant spider web made of wooden bridges spanning as far as the eye could see. Arborville was an entire village in the trees.

"The bridges are essentially our version of roads," Ethan explained. "They link our homes and shops together. We can travel without setting foot on the ground. It's safer in the tree canopy. Any lemerons passing by remain unaware of our presence. And if they do become aware, they can't climb, so we're safe."

"It's amazing," Jennie said. "Who built all this?"

Ethan scrunched up his face. "I don't know who had the idea to build the first treehouses. They've always been here as far as I know. When the older houses have wood that starts to rot, we replace the planks with newer wood. Some of the oldest treehouses have been rebuilt multiple times, one board at a time."

Ethan pointed ahead of them.

"Over there is where the newer houses are. As our population grows, we build new houses in the outer trees. When the floor is finished, we build a bridge to connect it with the rest of Arborville."

"Do you help build the houses?"

"Well, I don't. Not exactly. I've helped with repairs from time to time, but I usually spend my days hunting and scouting." He shrugged. "I guess it's kind of like in the Commune, we all have our specialties."

Jennie gazed up at Arborville. She noticed a second level of houses above the ones lower to the ground. She squinted, trying to see better in the fading light of dusk. Around some larger trees, it looked like there was a third level of buildings even higher up.

"You build up as well as out?" she asked.

"Yes. Some trees aren't strong enough to support so many structures, so we just build what we can and where we can."

"This is amazing," Jennie said.

"It's even more incredible from higher up," Ethan stepped next to a nearby tree. "Come on, let me show you."

Beside him, hanging from the platform above, was a ladder. It was made up of two long segments of rope with narrow wood planks tied between them. The rope was frayed in places where presumably years of use took its toll.

"After you," he said.

She placed a tentative hand on the ladder. It swayed from her touch. She bit her lower lip, forgetting it was still healing. Putting her foot on a plank, she shifted her weight off the ground. The ropes trembled as much as she did.

She much preferred the solid wood ladder in her barn. She climbed up and down it for years. But it never moved like this one. Placing a foot on the next rung, her weight shifted, and the ladder pushed away from her.

"I don't know if I can do this," she cried out.

"You can do it." Ethan held the rope on either side of her. "Let me help."

His steadying grip made it easier. Jennie wanted to get this over with. She longed for a chair to sit and a stool to prop up her feet. Taking a deep breath, she climbed.

One rung after another, up she went. When she reached the top, someone extended a hand to her. She took it blindly.

Their palm was callused and rough, and their grip strong. She stepped onto a solid platform and pressed her back against the tree trunk jutting out from the middle of it.

"Thank you," she said to the stranger.

He was short with broad shoulders and a bald head. His brown tunic and pants made him look like a walking tree stump. Something about his appearance reminded her of Sash. Only he was a lot shorter, and smile lines etched his face.

"Welcome. It's not often we see a fresh face around here. I'm Chaz, one of the sentries. Who might you be?"

"Jennie." Her voice came out small and squeaky.

She tugged at the ends of her sleeves. First meeting Ethan had been shocking. Now she was in his treetop town. Each person out here was more evidence of the lies the Order fed her people. They said there was no one left alive beyond the wall. Chaz was more proof of their deception.

Ethan swiftly climbed the ladder and joined her on the platform.

"Making friends already, I see. Thanks for the rope, Chaz. It's just the two of us. Did my..." Ethan's voice broke off. He cleared his throat before continuing. "Did anyone else arrive?"

He's asking about Marlene, Jennie realized.

"No, not by my watch. Chester was on lookout last night. Ya might want to check with him."

Ethan's face fell.

"Yeah, sure, I'll do that," he said.

Jennie's heart went out to him. She knew what it was like to lose a mother. He never knew his. She abandoned him when he was just a baby.

It was still strange to Jennie that one of the Commune's Elders, Marlene, was Ethan's mother. She knew his mother her whole life. It didn't seem right that Jennie knew more of her than Ethan. But now, he had this opportunity to reunite with her. Jennie wanted to help see it through for his sake. She lost a mother; it felt right to help Ethan find his.

"Come on, Jennie, let's get some warmth and food before we track down Chester."

Ethan's eyes glistened with tears in the fading light. He turned away and hurried off.

She glanced from Chaz to Ethan and back to Chaz. He scrunched his face in confusion, as though wondering if he said something wrong.

"It's been a long and dangerous journey. We both could use some rest. Thanks again for your help."

She rushed after Ethan, the suspension bridge bouncing underfoot. She held on to the rope railing to keep her balance.

"Anytime," Chaz called after her.

Ethan rubbed his eyes with the back of his hand. Without looking at her, he said, "I'm sorry about that. It's just -- it's just a lot to come to terms with. I still don't know how to deal with the idea of meeting the woman who left me for dead in the woods."

"It's okay. You don't have to apologize to me. This isn't an easy thing to do. Especially not after the past few days we've had."

He lowered his head. "Yeah, you're right. Let's just eat and get some sleep. We'll worry about it tomorrow."

Ethan walked on, taking one suspension bridge after another. He stopped at a treehouse grander than any of the others Jennie saw. The tree they built it around was thicker and taller than any others nearby. At two stories tall, the building was massive. Her entire house could fit inside this one at least four times. Granted, her house was small. Something delicious was cooking inside. The smell wafted out through the cracked door.

Her stomach growled.

"This is our main hall. We should find some food in here."

Ethan held the door open for Jennie. Tentatively, she stepped inside the round building. It was bright and warm with woven rugs covering the floor. Chairs and tables were arranged around the room in various seating arrangements. A staircase leading to the second story spiraled around the thick tree trunk in the middle of the room. An old woman stirred something in a cauldron placed over a fire.

It was amazing they could have a fire inside a structure made entirely of wood. But they had built a proper stone hearth and fireplace along the outside wall of the treehouse. Jennie took a step closer to the woman. She looked up. The wrinkles in her face became more pronounced as she flashed a toothless smile.

"Hello there, dear. Have you come for a late supper?" The old woman asked in a crackling voice.

Jennie peered into the pot. Mouthwatering chunks of meat and vegetables floated in a thick broth. She licked her lips. She wanted to eat whatever this woman was cooking, but she wasn't sure if she was allowed to. Glancing over her shoulder at Ethan, he nodded, letting her know it was okay.

"Yes, please," Jennie said.

"Good. The stew is perfect. Any longer over the fire and the potatoes will turn to mush," she smacked her lips. "Although, that works for me just fine."

She laughed heartily, her pink gums visible. The old

woman took two bowls and spoons down from a shelf and ladled the chunky stew into them. She handed one each to Jennie and Ethan. "Thanks, Old Nan," Ethan said.

Jennie walked to a plush chair as fast as she dared, careful not to spill her meal. She lowered herself into the soft cushions with a sigh. It was such a relief to get off her aching feet. Scarfing down the stew in silence, she savored every bite. It was rich and flavorful. After starving for days, this was one of the best meals she ever had.

Ethan gobbled his bowl up, too.

She heard footsteps just above them. Her eyes followed the sound of movement along the ceiling. They approached the spiral stairs, then descended the steps. Jennie could only see the back of a woman with long, blonde hair coming down.

Whoever it was, she looked like she been in a scrap recently. Her clothes were pretty beat up. She curved out of sight behind the tree trunk. Jennie heard the hollow thud as the woman stepped onto the floor.

Jennie returned to her bowl, scraping the last bits of broth up with her spoon.

The woman's footsteps came closer to her from behind. They stopped suddenly, followed by a familiar voice.

"Jennie? Is that you?"

Her breath caught in her throat when she turned and saw Marlene standing behind her.

FIFTEEN

Marlene
_____

"What are you doing here?" Marlene asked. "You're insane to leave the Commune. Don't you know about the endless threats in the wilderness?"

She wasn't sure if Arborville would still be standing by the time she arrived. With so many lemerons passing through to reach the Commune, she was sure they would have decimated the place. Yet to her immense relief, it remained untouched.

She arrived that morning and spent all day trying to find Ethan. She found out he was sent to investigate the increase in lemeron activity, but no one had seen him in weeks. Her unease grew the longer she looked in vein.

"Answer me, child," she snapped. "What are you doing here?"

Jennie shrank back in her chair. Marlene stepped square in front of her, hands on her hips. The knot in her stomach clenched tighter.

"Looking for you," she answered sheepishly.

Marlene frowned.

"Why would you be looking for me? I told you all I was going for help, didn't I?" She jabbed a finger at Jennie. "You should have stayed put. I'll be damned if some foolish girl gets killed simply because she was looking for me."

The girl shifted in her seat and clamped her mouth shut.

"I don't have time for this," Marlene waved a dismissive hand. "I'm searching for someone. Stay here or go back, it doesn't matter to me. Just try not to get killed."

She strode past the girl, making for the exit. Jennie was whispering something behind her back. Probably quietly cursing herself for her stupidity. Let her.

I have to find Ethan. If he's dead, I don't know if I could withstand the grief. Her chin trembled. *At least I would have closure.*

Marlene left him nearly eighteen years ago with his father, but there was always the lingering hope she might see him again. If he perished, everything she sacrificed would have been for nothing.

"Mother?" A young man's voice called from behind her.

She hesitated a moment. Surely, he wasn't talking to her. He was probably speaking to the woman cooking in the corner. But there was something familiar about his voice.

The floorboard creaked behind her. Whoever spoke was coming closer to her. Her heart pounded in her chest.

It can't be him. It's too much to hope for.

The floor creaked again as he took another step.

Turn around, she urged herself. And so she did.

She gasped, clasping a hand over her open mouth. Before her stood Brenden, only he was younger and had her eyes.

The last memory she had of her son flashed through her mind. He was a happy baby with those bright green eyes. She passed him over to his father. Her little boy wouldn't let go of her finger. He was strong then, and he looked to be even stronger now.

His muscular build was very much like his father's. Marlene extended her hand, tempted to touch his stubble covered jaw. The shape was a bit like her own jaw, slightly squared. Her fingers shook as they neared his face.

Her attention was pulled behind him, and she lowered her hand. Jennie stood there a few paces back, a smile plastered on her face. Marlene furrowed her brow.

Did she do this? Did she bring my son to me? How did Jennie come to know him?

Marlene focused on the young man before her. His eyes were glassy. His chest barely moved, as though he were holding his breath.

"Ethan?" Marlene asked, her voice shaking.

The young man sucked in air and exhaled rapidly. It almost came out as a laugh.

"Mother."

It was really him. Ethan was alive and well. Her little baby boy was all grown up.

"Oh, my son." She pulled him to her, wrapping her arms around him for the first time in eighteen years. And for the first time in nearly a hundred years, she cried.

SIXTEEN

Ethan

_____

"I can't believe I'm finally meeting you," Ethan said.

Marlene wrapped her arms around him, holding him close.

She smells like wild strawberries and pine needles. Like the forest.

She pulled away, gripping his shoulders in her hands. Her green eyes darted around his face, taking him in. Jennie was right, they had the same eyes. His mother looked exactly as she did in the picture of her in his pocket. When she abandoned him in the forest as a baby, she left that picture with him.

His eyes stung with tears that threatened to fall. He didn't want to cry in front of his mother… or Jennie. He bit his lower lip, fighting the urge to cry.

"Why did you leave me in the forest?" He asked.

Marlene's face fell, and she wiped her eyes with her finger. "We'll get to that later. Is there somewhere we can go to talk?"

Ethan glanced around the open hall, aware of the onlookers. The privacy of his home seemed like a good idea. He had so many questions for her.

He was angry with her for leaving him in the forest, but

happy to meet her. All his life, he thought she didn't want him. But here she was, crying with joy after seeing him. He was so conflicted. Every emotion possible was rushing through him, ripping him apart. He had to know more and work through these feelings. But not here, in front of a crowd. Home was best. Except his father would be there. Sooner or later, they would probably meet.

"I, uh, would like you to meet my father," Ethan ran a hand through his matted hair.

This was more awkward than he anticipated. Here he was meeting his birth mother for the first time, and he invites her to meet his adoptive father. What would she think of his father? He frowned. What would he think of her?

She left him alone in the forest as a baby. If his father hadn't come along, Ethan might have died out there. Come to think of it, he might not want to meet the woman who left her child for dead.

"I would like that," she said.

"He is my, um, adoptive father," Ethan chewed the inside of his cheeks. "He found me as a baby in the woods."

She pressed her lips together into a thin line and nodded.

He ran his hand through his hair again.

"All right then. Follow me, I guess."

He left the main hall, glancing over his shoulder to make sure Marlene and Jennie were behind him. His entire body tingled. While crossing the bridges connecting the treehouses, he felt clumsy like his feet were too large for his body.

He stumbled, losing his balance. Reaching out, he grabbed the rope railing of one of the bridges. His heart pounded in his chest. Clinging to the rope, he waited for the bridge to stop bobbing up and down. His stomach had that weird feeling again… butterflies.

Get it together, he told himself.

He looked back over his shoulder. His mother and Jennie

waited without saying a word. Taking a deep breath, he walked on.

After crossing a few more bridges, he finally reached the home he shared with his father. It was a modest house, but it was theirs. He stared at the weathered door.

When he was only nine, he wanted their house to have a blue door.

"Why blue?" his father asked.

"Because the sky is blue and we live in the sky," he said.

"Right you are," his father chuckled at his wit.

So, they went out hunting for blueberries until they had a bushel full. They spent the entire afternoon mashing them into a liquid and smearing it on the door. They used a crude brush Ethan made out of pine needles, twine, and a stick. It did the job well enough.

The door turned out to be more purple than blue.

Now only streaks of faded purple remained in the deeper grooves of the wood. He ran his hand down one of the more pronounced streaks.

His father was everything to him. He taught him everything he knew and made Ethan the man he was today.

What will he think about my birth mother?

It was too late to turn back.

He inhaled deeply, then exhaled, trying to slow his heartbeat. He pushed the door open and stepped inside.

His father was there, tending to the fire, his back to the door. He jerked his head up when he heard the door.

His father's face lit up the moment he laid eyes on him.

"Ethan, my boy," he exclaimed, approaching him with widespread arms.

Ethan couldn't even attempt a smile, he was so nervous. His father frowned, dropping his arms to his side.

"What's wrong? Ethan, did something happen? Tell me, what's the matter?"

He bit his lower lip and stepped aside, letting his mother and Jennie enter the house.

"I found my mother."

His father's mouth dropped open.

Marlene stepped around Ethan and approached his father. "Hello, Brenden."

Ethan shook his head. "How do you know his name?"

She reached out, stroking his father's cheek.

The butterflies turned to fire in his stomach. He felt like he might be sick.

Why is she touching him like that? She only just met him.

"Because he's my husband."

Ethan staggered back. He tripped over something and fell to the ground. All he could do was watch as Marlene and his father stood too close to each other.

"No. This is impossible," Ethan yelled. "You don't really know him. This is some cruel joke. Why are you doing this to me?"

Marlene turned to face Ethan, stepping closer to him. He scooted away from her on the floor, but his back met the wall. He was trapped.

"This is no joke, Ethan," she said. "Brenden is my husband, and he is your real father. He didn't adopt you, he sired you."

Her voice cut like cold daggers. The flames in his stomach turned to ice.

"No," he shook his head. "You're wrong. He *found* me. You left me in the woods to die."

She shot a glance at his father, then fixed her gaze on Ethan. "I left you in his arms. It wasn't safe for you to stay with me in the Commune. I handed you over to Brenden to keep you safe, which is exactly what he did."

He looked at his father. Tears welled in Ethan's eyes, not caring anymore if he cried. His whole life had been a deception.

"You're my *real* father? How could you not tell me? You let me live my entire life thinking my actual parents never wanted me." Ethan jabbed an accusing finger in his father's direction. "You let me believe that you were some stranger wandering through the forest when you just happened to find a baby who you raised as your adopted son. Why would you lie to me like that?"

The tears overflowed, streaming down his face.

"It would have been too painful to tell you the truth. It was hard enough losing your mother once, I couldn't bear talking about her. It would have been like losing her all over again. It was easier this way," Brendan said.

"Is that what you tell yourself so you can live with your lie?"

His father opened his mouth to speak. Ethan raised his hands, shaking his head.

"Don't answer that. I don't care what you have to say. Everything that comes out of your mouth is a lie. You lied to me my entire life. How could you?"

"Ethan, you have to understand, it was for the best," he tried to explain, but Ethan didn't want to hear it.

"Best for who?" He shouted. "You? Her?"

He pointed his finger at Marlene.

"Neither of you care about me. If you did, you would have told me the truth," he clambered to his feet. "I don't even know where I belong anymore. I just know it's not here."

He rushed from the house he once called home, slamming the purple-streaked door behind him.

SEVENTEEN

Jennie

_____

J ennie was stunned. She stood, glancing from Marlene to Brenden. No one said a word. The air in the one-room house was thick with tension.

A string tugged on her heart, urging her to go after Ethan. She wanted to, more than anything, but she had no idea where he went. This settlement was entirely foreign to her. She was disoriented as soon as they left the main hall.

Marlene crossed her arms and pursed her lips at Jennie as if silently saying this was all her fault. It wasn't, though. How could it be?

All she wanted was to see Ethan happy. She thought he would want to be reunited with his mother. And he did... until he found out just how deep their lies go. Jennie never could have expected his adoptive father turned out to be his actual father.

Brenden, was staring at Jennie, too. Only his expression was less accusing than Marlene's.

She wrung her cold hands together, trying to warm them, but also to steady her nerves. The silence was overwhelming. No one said anything, but so many questions hung in the air.

It seemed that if she didn't speak up, no one would. She

swallowed hard, mustering her courage to ask her burning question.

"What just happened?"

Marlene closed her eyes, shaking her head. When she finally opened them, she spoke in a frigid tone.

"You interfered, that's what happened."

Jennie was taken aback. "What? Me?"

"If you hadn't had meddled, Ethan would still think Brenden adopted him," her face spasmed with pain. "It would have been better if Ethan never met me."

"I'm confused, you're saying Ethan getting upset because you both lied to him was my fault?"

"I had to know Ethan was alive and okay. I could have done that from afar, without meeting him," Marlene said. "You told him who I was, didn't you? You shouldn't have. It would have been better if he still believed Brenden's story." She looked at him with longing in her eyes.

Jennie felt her face turn hot. Her blood was boiling. No one accused her of something she didn't do. Not even a Commune Elder. She stepped up to Marlene, staring her right in the eye.

"You were the one who got all touchy-feely with his father. That obviously upset Ethan. You should have told him everything back at the hall instead of letting him think you didn't know his father."

Brenden stepped forward. "I'm sorry, but who are you?"

Marlene answered for her. "Her name is Jennie Caraway. She's from the Commune and a known troublemaker."

Jennie crossed her arms. "Why? Because I told you your inaction gave the Order the room they needed to destroy the Commune from the inside out? If you would have just done *something* before things got out of hand, we might not have hundreds of lemerons just outside our walls."

Marlene's lip twitched. Her eyes flashed with anger.

Jennie took a step back. She said something to hit a nerve. She never saw Marlene so furious. Ever.

"Those monsters took everything from me!" Her nostrils flared. "I lost my friends, my family, and any chance I had for a normal life."

"But now you have a chance to get it back," Jennie said.

"It's far too late for that."

"Then why are you really here? You abandoned the Commune in a state of chaos that you helped create. You said you were leaving to find help. Was that just another lie?"

"No. That was part of my reason for leaving. I came here to make sure Ethan was okay. But now, he wants nothing to do with Brenden or me. No thanks to you," Marlene added.

"He's just upset. He'll get over it, he just needs a little time," Jennie said.

"There are some wounds time can't heal, trust me. This is one of them," Marlene said.

Jennie shook her head. She had enough of her stubbornness. "Just because you've lived a freakishly long time, you think you know everything. You both just gave Ethan earth-shattering news and all in the same night." Jennie pointed to Marlene. "And now you would just abandon Ethan to fend for himself? Again?"

"Ethan rejected me, so be it. I don't have time to wait around for someone to *maybe* change their mind. I have more important things to worry about, like the lemerons you're always so concerned about."

Jennie scoffed. She couldn't believe how cold Marlene was. "So, just like that, you would sacrifice your relationship with your son?"

Marlene slammed her fist against the tree trunk in the middle of the room. The house shook from the impact. "I would sacrifice *everything* to stop the lemerons."

Brenden placed a hand on her shoulder. "Marlene, the girl

is just trying to understand my decision about how to raise Ethan."

Jennie glared at him. "You should have told Ethan you're his father. He deserved to know the truth."

"You wouldn't understand such things, you're too young," Marlene cut in.

"I'm not a child anymore. I'm an adult, and I understand perfectly well."

"Your actions say otherwise," Marlene said.

"Well, I will do something you've chosen not to and actually be there for Ethan."

Jennie turned on her heel and left the house. She slammed the door behind her to drive her point home. She would cross every bridge in this place until she found Ethan.

Standing alone on the platform outside the door, she took in her surroundings. The stars were out now, peeking through the leaves. Lights coming from the treehouses made it look like the stars also lived amongst the trees. It was beautiful.

The night air was still and quiet with an owl hooting in the distance. Had the drama not unfolded behind the door at her back, she would feel at peace here. Ethan deserved better. She would be distraught too if she were in his place.

A chopping sound came from the trees to her right. It sounded like someone splitting firewood.

Could that be Ethan?

Drawn to the chopping sound, she followed her ears. She had to cross the suspension bridges slowly. She could hardly see where she was putting her feet. She didn't want to miss a step and fall to the ground below. That would be a long way to drop.

She saw movement ahead. A shadowy figure of a man was hacking at a tree trunk with what looked like a machete. Tentatively, she crept closer. She didn't want to surprise someone in the dark, swinging a blade. With each strike from the machete, chips of bark flew into the air.

The man let out a roar and slashed at the tree with so much force, Jennie could see the blade bite deep into the trunk. He tugged at the handle, trying to pull it free, but it was stuck.

Giving up, the man raised his fists above his head and pounded the tree. He rested his head against the trunk.

Jennie heard him sob and took another step closer. This had to be Ethan. Who else would be out here alone at night, taking their frustration out on a tree?

"Ethan?" She put a tentative hand on his shoulder.

He tensed, spinning around brandishing his fists.

Jennie's heart leapt to her throat. She held up her hands in surrender, stepping backward. She lost her footing and tripped. She cried out as she fell, afraid she would fall off the edge of the platform.

A muscular hand grabbed her arm and pulled her back to her feet. The man pulled her close, wrapping his arms around her. She was shaking in his arms. Finally, she looked up to see who the mystery man really was.

Ethan's emerald eyes, wet with tears, peered down at her.

"I'm so sorry," he kissed her forehead. "I didn't mean to scare you. For a moment, I thought you were a lemeron."

"It's okay. I'm okay." Jennie frowned, wondering about the monsters. "Can they get up here?"

"No. I just forgot where I was." He let go of her and turning back to the tree. "I forgot who I was."

Jennie's heart broke in half for him.

"I came to check on you and make sure you're okay."

Ethan shook his head. "It was a mistake to come back here. I should have known having a real mother was too good to be true." He spun back around to face her. "Let's leave."

"And go back to the Commune?" Jennie asked.

"No. Let's leave it all behind and find somewhere new. Our two settlements can't be the only ones left in the world. Let's find who else might be out there."

Jennie reached out, taking his hands in hers.

"It's late. We're both tired and sore. I'm sure we both could use a good night's sleep. In the morning, we'll figure out what's next."

As much as she would enjoy going on an adventure with Ethan under normal circumstances, that was probably the worst thing he could do right now. He wanted to run from his problems. Like it or not, he had to face them. He had to face his parents.

EIGHTEEN

Belle

Travis needs more time to calm down.

Belle didn't try to approach him. He was still upset with her. If she needed to find him, she knew where to look. For the past three days, he'd been living at the stables. Remaining out of sight, she kept an eye on him there from the apple orchard.

How strange that her best friend's safe haven from the world had now become Travis's. Jennie would often retreat there if she was troubled. She always told Belle that no one ever bothered her there. The horses were a comfort to her.

I guess Travis needs the same kind of comfort right now. We've all been through so much.

Doubting his father and Belle losing her cool with him probably didn't help.

As much as she loved Jennie, she found working with animals stressful because of how much they depended on you. You could fail them just as easily as people.

She preferred working on the solar panels. On days like this, when the weather was cooler and the clouds drifted overhead, it was perfect. Except today, it wasn't. She wasn't sure if it ever would be again.

She sat in the grass hunched over her toolbox, stripping a replacement wire.

Usually, work helped take her mind off things, but it wasn't working today. Every time she heard something behind her, she thought it was Sash coming for her. Her heart would stop and she would spin around only to see a squirrel scampering about. She could still feel the prick of the needle in her arm and the black sack being pulled over her head. If Sash showed up again, no one could save her this time.

Jennie and Ethan were gone. Travis was a thirteen-year-old kid with a good heart, but he couldn't overpower Sash. Who else would help?

She couldn't focus. She cut and stripped the same wire over and over again. Each time she stripped it, she cut through too many of the copper strands, so she'd have to trim it and start over. Every time she messed up, it got shorter. At this rate, she wouldn't have any wire left.

"It's useless!"

She threw the wire remnant on the ground and slammed the lid of her toolbox shut. Returning to her locker, she shoved her tools inside and locked it.

Belle made her way back to the town square. Maybe she could pass her time watching the birds play in the fountain.

A cold wind blew, messing up her curls. She shivered. Over the past few days, it had been too quiet in the Commune. It was midday, and no one was out on the streets. Usually, people would be out shopping, conversing, or tending the plants in their garden beds. But no one was around.

Everything had gone awry since Jennie left. They were a society filled with fear and without elders. Those who used to stop in the streets to say hello now scurried away from anyone they saw. It didn't matter who.

Belle understood it. No one knew who was part of the

Order. They could live next door, and you would never know. Everyone was a suspect to everyone else.

The atmosphere is so rigid, it could snap at any moment. When that happens, chaos will take over. Panic will ensue. Is that what the Order wants?

The more lemerons that gathered outside the wall, the more their decaying stench filled the air. The Commune was a pot of water slowly coming to a boil. It was about to bubble over.

She reached the edge of town as the schoolhouse bell started tolling. Someone was calling an assembly.

"Now what?" She groaned.

She filed inside the central Sanctuary building just like everyone else. No one spoke or acknowledged each other, almost like a pack of dociles.

So, this is what fear does to a society.

Normally, there would be at least some idle chatter in the crowd, but no one said a word. On the other side of the room, someone coughed. Belle shook her head. This was too much. People needed to snap out of it. There was a war to fight outside the Commune, and no one was lifting a finger. They were too afraid of the dangers within the walls to do anything at all.

The chairs in the grand chamber slowly filled. It seemed to take hours for everyone to arrive. Belle shifted uncomfortably in her seat.

When the doors slammed shut, she whipped her head around to see who closed them. She frowned.

A man strode up the length of the central aisle. His face and eyes were battered with purplish-green bruises. There was something about him that looked familiar.

Where have I seen him before?

The Commune was small enough that most people knew each other, but this man wasn't someone she knew. But she had seen him. And recently, too.

She shifted again. There was something wrong about him.

The man's footsteps echoed as he climbed the platform at the front of the room.

"My fellow citizens, thank you for coming," he said.

His voice was gruff but Belle didn't recognize it. He scanned the room through his bruised eyes. One of them was swollen half shut.

"Some of you may know me, for those of you who don't, I'm Isaac Fenske."

Now Belle had a name to go with the face, but the name wasn't familiar to her.

"We've been living together our entire lives, but recently the balance of our society was thrown into chaos. Marlene abandoned us, and Victor betrayed us."

That's not right. Belle frowned. *Marlene went to get help. She didn't abandon us.*

"We are afraid of each other when we should be afraid of the lemerons at the wall. Our friends and neighbors aren't a threat. Those monsters at our gates are. We must rise up together and fight for our survival."

A few people in the crowd murmured their agreement. Belle wanted to agree too, but something about him was off.

"We don't have anyone to lead us through this nightmare. This situation is unprecedented. That's why I humbly ask your approval to let me stand in as an interim Elder until two new Elders are selected. If you consent, say 'aye.'"

Two new Elders? Marlene was coming back. What was he playing at? Only Victor needed replacing.

The room was silent. Belle scanned the crowd, wondering if anyone would answer his plea for power. Nearby, a few people were conversing with each other. She couldn't hear what they were saying, but they were both nodding.

One of them looked up and shouted, "aye."

The other one echoed him with an "aye."

Throughout the room, more people were adding their

"ayes" to the chorus. The people in the room came alive with new hope.

That's when it hit her. Belle's eyes grew wide, and she felt the color drain from her face. She remembered where she saw him.

This man, Isaac Fenske, was lying unconscious and bloody on a table in Goggles's lab. She remembered seeing him before the fight with Sash. She hadn't been sure if he was alive or dead when they left him behind during their escape.

He was very much alive now. How did *he* manage to escape?

There was something about him, and this sudden grab for power which made Belle think of Victor. This was a move someone from the Order would make. But what could she do without proof? She only had her suspicions.

Jennie's parting words echoed in her mind: *do what you can to keep the Order out of power.*

A smile tugged at the corners of Isaac's mouth.

"Anyone opposed to my proposition, say 'nay.'"

Belle whispered so only she could hear. "Nay."

NINETEEN

Travis
___

Travis rushed out of the assembly hall and down the front steps of the Sanctuary building. He had to get to Belle. Where would she be?

I got so caught up on her causing drama between me and my father, I lost sight of the bigger problem: the Order.

Who was this Isaac guy, anyway? Travis was thirteen now, so he could vote on decisions such as this… at least he thought he could. If Jennie were there, she would have told him how these things work.

He didn't know for sure, so he remained silent. What would he have said? He didn't know enough about Isaac to say aye. He also didn't know enough about him to say nay.

Maybe this guy will do good things for the Commune, as he promised.

Travis had to talk through this with someone. Belle seemed like the best person. He also needed to apologize to her for how sour he'd been. She had a bit of a temper, that was all. She was just sticking up for him, after all.

"Travis," someone whispered behind him.

He spun around and grinned.

"Belle. I'm so glad you found me. I was looking for you. Look, I'm sorry about -"

"It doesn't matter," she cut him off, keeping her voice low. "We messed up. Big time."

The smile fell from his face. He rubbed his sweaty palms on his pants.

"What do you mean?" He asked, afraid of the answer. It was bad news, based on the concern etched on her face.

"We can't speak here. Come with me."

They crossed the square and entered the apothecary shop. The little bell hanging above the door jingled. The aromatic scent of herbs and spices was a welcome one. It was a major improvement from the smell of rotting flesh outside. Countless little drawers and bottles filled nearly the entire wall behind the counter.

"Why are we here?" Travis whispered.

"Uncle Albert. Jennie said we can trust him, remember?"

"Well, yeah."

It was obvious they could. Uncle Albert was the person Travis sought out after the tensions with his father and Belle. He spent a good deal of time here after that fight. Uncle Albert calmed him down and assured him father was one of the Truth Seekers.

The knot in his stomach unraveled at that news. Even with the confirmation that his father was one of the good guys, he still couldn't bring himself to go home. He needed some space to clear his head.

A little old man opened a creaky door behind the shop counter. He stepped over the threshold and closed the door behind him. He peered at them through the round lenses of his glasses.

"What can I do for you two today? How about a little dried mint to add to your morning tea? It will help settle your stomach if you feel queasy from the smell outside."

Travis and Belle exchanged a curious look. Was this some

sort of prompt for a secret password only Truth Seekers know?

"None of that, thanks. We need to talk about other business." Belle got straight to the point.

Uncle Albert pursed his wrinkled lips.

"I see." He glanced through the window behind them. "Did anyone see you enter the shop?"

"I don't think so," Travis said.

"Well then, hurry on back before anyone sees you standing there," Uncle Albert said.

He shuffled to the end of the counter and lifted a section up. It swung open on a set of hinges like a horizontal doorway.

Travis and Belle stepped through the opening. There were even more bottles and drawers hidden behind the counter, each one filled with herbs, medicines, and tonics. A spool of twine was next to a stack of paper.

I guess that's what Uncle Albert uses to bundle up things people buy.

The old man lowered the counter, letting it fall the last few inches with a thud.

"This way." He opened the short door he had come through earlier.

Travis and Belle had to duck to avoid bumping their heads on the top of the door frame. Uncle Albert walked through without issue. He closed the door behind him, barring it shut from the inside.

Travis swallowed. The last time he was here, the old man didn't lock the door.

"What's changed since I was here last?" He asked. "Is someone going to break in and attack us?"

"Nothing more than precautions," Uncle Albert said.

Travis blinked a few times, trying to adjust his eyes to the dim light in the back room. It smelled even more potent than the front of the shop. The overpowering scent of mint made his eyes water and nostrils burn. His nose twitched and he sneezed loudly into his arm.

"Uh, sorry," he wiped his nose with his sleeve. Nothing came out, but his nose still felt gross.

Uncle Albert mumbled something as he lit a few candles. The old man crossed his arms.

"Next time use the side door," he scolded.

"Sorry, I didn't know," Belle said.

"Uh… I forgot. Sorry." Travis dropped his gaze to his feet.

Uncle Albert studied them for a moment through his glasses. He sat down in an old chair at the head of a table.

"Just remember for next time." He gestured for them to sit.

Belle and Travis sat at the table.

"I heard the bells calling the Commune Council meeting. These old bones don't let me attend any more. Now tell me, what's this all about?"

"I think someone from the Order may have just been elected as an interim elder," Belle said.

Uncle Albert took his glasses off and rubbed his eyes. He looked much older than Travis remembered. It had only been a few days since he saw him last, but something was weighing heavily on him.

"I see," he said wearily. "What makes you think he, or she, is part of the Order?"

"I saw him in the underground lab where they turn people into dociles," Belle leaned in as she spoke.

"What was his condition?"

"He was beat up pretty badly and unconscious."

"Why do you think that makes him part of the Order? It makes him sound like one of their victims."

Travis nodded. That was a good point. Maybe Belle was just worried for nothing.

"Does the name Isaac Fenske mean anything to you?" She asked.

Air hissed through Uncle Albert's nostrils. He replaced his glasses and studied her, hard.

"I know the name Isaac Fenske well, but he is *not* one of us. Your intuition is right, young lady. Isaac is part of the Order. If he's now taken control in the Commune, we're all in trouble."

Belle leaned back in her chair, her face pale.

"Well, crap," she said.

Travis swallowed. This wasn't good.

TWENTY

Sash

_____

"They believed you?" Sash asked.

Isaac stroked his chin. "Certainly. People are so afraid that their own mother or brother might be part of the Order, they failed to recognize someone who actually is. No one opposed me, and no one volunteered to stand in as the other interim elder. Fear and a compelling speech are powerful motivators. We have the Commune under our complete control."

Sash sneered. Isaac was teaching Sash that goals could be accomplished without brute force. He never would have thought it possible.

Although, he craved the way it felt to punch someone. He rubbed the knuckles of his fist, imagining the sensation of hitting an undesirable.

"When will you make your next move?"

Sash was eager to know when he could help above ground. He was tired of sitting in Goggles's office every day watching through the window while the weird scientist worked in the lab.

"Soon. We can't rush these things. I won the vote today.

Now I need to win the people's unwavering trust." Isaac laughed.

Sash frowned. *Did I miss a joke?*

"What's so funny?"

"A man came up to me before everyone dispersed and asked what happened to my face."

"Did you tell him I attacked you?"

"No. The truth is always so bland. I told him Victor had a group of men attack me when I found out about his deceptions. I accomplished two things with that statement." Isaac held up a finger. "One, starting a rumor that there are groups of people with the Order roaming the streets attacking others, and two," he raised another finger, "conveying that I am more of a victim than anyone else, yet I stand for the people."

"I see." Sash scratched his bald head.

"Oh, but that's not the best part. I've got a little treat for you." He clapped his hands together.

Sash looked up to see Goggles enter the lab through the door to the docile corridor. That was where he kept those undergoing processing and those next in line for it. He was pushing something. Sash stood to get a better look. His eyes grew wide, and his nostrils flared.

"How did you get him from the undesirables?"

"It turns out once you're an elder, no one asks you why you're moving a prisoner or where to. Especially when it's this prisoner."

Goggles rolled the table into position beneath the bright lights in the lab. Victor struggled against the straps holding him down. He had a gag in his mouth, so he couldn't speak, but it didn't stop him from making noise.

Sash narrowed his eyes at the man who used him for his entire adult life.

"You want me to torture him for information?" He asked.

"Heavens no. That would be pointless. He's lied to you

and manipulated you for years. He'll just try the same tactics again. Everything he says will be a lie."

Sash narrowed his gaze at Victor. "I can be very persuasive."

"I don't doubt it for a moment. I've got something better in mind, though."

Intrigued, he turned his back on Victor to face Isaac. "What do you need me to do?"

"I want you to get your closure with Victor," Isaac said, his tone serious. "I want you to process him."

Sash was stunned. "You're asking me to turn him into a docile. Why?"

Isaac peered through the window at the deposed elder squirming on the table. "Because it's the right thing to do," he answered. "This man has used you for far too long. It's time you return the favor and put him to use."

Sash blinked slowly. "You're right. Victor has taken advantage of my loyalty and used me. I tracked down our enemies and killed them or brought them here for processing. What was it all for? I gave everything to Victor and got nothing in return. He's the true undesirable."

Isaac's lips twitched into a fleeting smile. "If anyone ever deserved to be processed, it's Victor."

"I'll do it," Sash said.

Isaac placed a reassuring hand on his shoulder. "Good. I know this will help you get closure so you can move forward with the rest of us."

Sash stepped through the door from the office into the lab. Goggles had the tray of processing chemicals drawn up into syringes, ready to go. Sash had seen him perform this procedure multiple times before. Sash was sure he could manage it himself. And if he screwed it up and things went wrong, Victor would die. One way or another, he'd be rid of this treacherous man.

Victor's grey eyes locked onto his. He mumbled something through the gag, squirming on the table. Sash ignored him and picked up the first syringe filled with green fluid. Removing the cap, he squirted some liquid out of the needle.

On the table, Victor's eyes grew wide. He thrashed around on the table, trying in vain to resist his fate.

Sash sneered, glad Victor understood what would happen to him. "It's your turn for processing." He jammed the needle into Victor's neck.

TWENTY-ONE

Travis

"This is a disaster," Belle said. "What can we do? Can we vote anyone else in as an interim elder? I mean, Marlene is gone, and Victor's out of the picture. So, what if Isaac is the stand-in for Marlene, and then we elect someone to replace Victor? That way, when Marlene gets back, she can kick Isaac out of his position. He probably thinks he'll permanently replace Victor, but maybe we can stop it."

"A fine suggestion. Who would you put to the vote?" Uncle Albert asked.

Belle shrugged. "I don't know. How about you or Mr. Caraway?"

Travis raised his eyebrows at the mention of his father. "My father won't do it. He keeps to himself, does his work, and keeps his head down. He doesn't want to lead anyone."

"I'm far too old and feeble for such a position," Uncle Albert said.

Belle scoffed. "Aren't you the leader of the Truth Seekers? If you can do that and keep it a secret, surely you can lead everyone else out in the open."

Uncle Albert shook his head. "It's not possible. Even if I were to stand, I wouldn't get the votes. No one will put their safety into the hands of an old man who can't fight off a mouse, let alone a lemeron." He tapped his chin thoughtfully. "However, your other suggestion holds merit. Jack Caraway would make a suitable candidate."

"Trust me, he won't do it," Travis said.

Uncle Albert stared at him. The candlelight in the dim storage room reflecting off the old man's glasses.

"Of all the people in the Commune, who stood up and took action when Marlene exposed Victor? Your father. Every single person saw him take a stand and do what was right. Removing an elder from power is extremely difficult, and few have ever even tried or had cause to. But your father did and succeeded. People will remember that."

Travis crossed his arms. "He's even more stubborn than Jennie. He's only focused on protecting himself, me, and Jennie. Everyone else doesn't matter. He only got upset when he found out Jennie got kidnapped and tortured. Sorry Belle, but you going through the same thing just didn't affect him as much. Truth Seeker or not, he wouldn't make a good choice."

Uncle Albert frowned.

The old man tisked, shaking his head. "This is a war, Travis. Wars are never without casualties. I lament what happened to both Belle and your sister. Your father does too, even if he didn't say it. The point is, we are so accustomed to working in secret that we sometimes lose sight of others' suffering."

He turned to Belle. "I'm sorry for what Sash and the Order put you through, Belle. You never should have been caught in the middle of this."

She brushed her long curls over her shoulder and shrugged. "Thanks, I guess."

"Here's what you two must do. Go to Jack and tell him he will stand as the second interim elder. The Commune must always have two. Isaac is not known to many, but he is an even greater threat than Victor," he turned to Travis. "Your father is well known and respected. He's an honorable man. If he is elected, he can obstruct Isaac's plans, whatever they may be."

"Then let's go tell him," Belle said. "We've waited too long to act, and things are getting worse. Come on, Travis."

She stood, the candles flickering as she hurried to the door.

"Not that way, dear," Uncle Albert called out. "The back door, please. With the eyes of the Order watching, we need to maintain our precautions."

"Right, sorry," she shied away from the door.

Uncle Albert rose from his chair. "I'll show you out."

He shuffled through the dim room until he reached the other side. He slid a metal rod over, unbarring the side door. It opened into a narrow room with hooks on the wall. A tan, tattered coat hung on one. The space looked more like a closet than anything else.

"Through there, it leads to the side street." He motioned to another door at the end of the little room.

"Thank you," Belle said.

"Yes, thanks, Uncle Albert," Travis added. "We'll go to my father now and tell him."

The old man nodded. After they stepped through to the coatroom, he closed the door behind them. Travis heard the bar sliding back in place, locking them out.

Things on the street were quiet. Travis looked to the left towards the main square. People were out, even chatting with each other. At a glance, things seemed almost normal again. He couldn't hear what they were saying, but their faces were calm, their bodies relaxed. A lady gestured playfully as she spoke to a man. It looked like she was flirting with him. Travis scrunched up his nose.

"This is too weird."

"What's that?" Belle asked.

"Look at them. Only this morning, everyone was afraid to

look at each other, and now they don't have a care in the world? They're acting like Isaac will fix everything."

"You're right. None of them know how dangerous the man they just elected is. Hell, we hardly do ourselves. At least we know he's dangerous," she frowned. "Uncle Albert said he's worse than Victor. That alone makes me feel sick to my stomach."

"Yeah. And the stench of the lemerons at the wall doesn't help. If that's Victor's doing, what will Isaac do?"

Belle mumbled something Travis couldn't quite make out.

"What?"

She shook her head. "Nothing. Let's just go deliver that message."

Turning on her heel, she walked away from the square. Travis glanced back at the fountain. A group of women laughed as they strolled by the stone horses spewing water.

How can they suddenly be so calm?

His father would at least try to do the right thing. Maybe it would do everyone good if he were an elder.

As Travis told his father about Uncle Albert's message, Jack simply sat there. There was no reaction or hint of what he was thinking. He just stared at his hands, clasped together on the kitchen table.

Silence filled the room when Travis stopped speaking. His father didn't say anything. Belle nudged Travis in the side.

"Will he do it?" She whispered out of the side of her mouth.

He shrugged and shook his head at the same time.

Jack just sat there, looking at his hands. His thumb twitched. He closed his eyes, taking a deep breath. He finally spoke. "For the good of the Commune, I'll do it."

TWENTY-TWO

Belle
—————

This time, she rang the bell. It was something Belle always wanted to do, but she'd never had the opportunity. Until now.

As a little girl, she wondered what the inside of the bell tower looked like. It rose from the pitched roof of the school next to the Sanctuary. She imagined that from up there you could see for hundreds of miles. She always thought the inside of the tower must hold secret passages and trap doors built into the spiral stairs.

When Travis's father asked if she could go ring the bell, she seized the opportunity. On her way, she nearly skipped with glee across the town square. She felt like a child again, living out one of her many dreams.

When she got inside, she was disappointed. Instead of a spiral staircase, there was a boring ladder. There were no secret passages, just old brick walls. And the only trap door was at the top of the ladder that opened to the outside. She crawled through onto the platform. The large bell hung suspended from the roof above her. The bell tower looking nothing like how she imagined it. What a waste.

Swallowing her disappointment, she gripped the tattered

rope and pulled. The brass bell tolled. It was so loud right next to it, her chest vibrated from the sound.

Belle leaned over the side of the platform to see people walking to the assembly hall in the Sanctuary building. They all looked so small from up here.

Making sure everyone heard, she pulled the rope again. When the bell grew silent, her ears still rang. She rubbed them, trying to quiet the lingering sound.

She climbed back down the ladder and left the schoolhouse.

As she walked through the halls, she worried that at any moment, one of the doors would fly open, and a teacher would chastise her for not being in class. She expected to hear sounds coming from within the classrooms. Teachers lecturing, students chattering, something. All she could hear was the sound of her footsteps echoing in the empty hall on the second floor.

Something was off. Approaching one of the classroom doors, she gripped the knob. Slowly turning it, she released the latch. Her arm was tense as she cracked the door open to peer inside.

There was no one there. Maybe this class wasn't in session. She went to the next door, opening it in the same manner. Again, the room was empty. Room after room revealed itself in the same abandoned state.

She furrowed her brow. She had only just rung the bell, calling an assembly. There wasn't enough time for everyone to leave the school. It had only been a couple minutes.

The strange thing was, there were no books, papers, or other school supplies on the students' desks. If they had just stepped out to go to the Sanctuary next door, they would have left their work in place. But the desks were clean.

"What in the world is going on here?" Belle asked herself.

She was answered by a footstep echoing from the far end of the hall. Her heart skipped a beat. In a vacant school, no one should be there. But someone was. Whoever was there took another step. And another. They were coming closer.

She heard a classroom door creak open. Peeking into the hall, she caught a glimpse of a black pant leg and shoe disappearing into a room down the hall. Her stomach plummeted to her feet. The person disappeared too quickly to know for sure who it might be, but she guessed it was someone from the Order.

Belle dashed to the stairs throwing the door open. It crashed against the hall, echoing like a crack of thunder. Her heart was racing twice as fast as her feet as she flew down the stairs.

From the second floor, she heard footsteps crashing after her. She reached the bottom of the steps and threw the door open, emerging into the first-floor corridor. Thankful for the flat surface, she ran faster. Taking a left, she dashed down a side hall leading to the back door.

Footsteps thundered down the stairs. He almost caught up to her. She flung open the back door, emerging into the sunlight. Catching the door before it could slam shut, she turned the knob and closed it softly. When the door was flush with the doorframe, she released the knob with a faint click.

Her heart was pounding in her throat. She tried to steady her breathing as she rushed along the back of the school. She spotted a group of girls coming down the adjacent street. She timed it so she could join them and blend in.

Belle rounded the corner and jogged a couple steps to join the other girls.

"Hey, you look out of breath. Afraid you might be late?" one girl asked her.

"Yeah, trying not to be," Belle said, adding silently, *or getting caught.*

The other girl nodded. "Us too. Looks like nearly everyone else might already be inside. We're here, though, so no need to worry."

After they entered the Sanctuary, Belle spotted some of her classmates already seated in the student section.

She broke off from the group and slid in next to her classmate on the bench.

"Hey, Mitch," she whispered.

"Hey," he whispered back. "Where have you been?"

"I've been sick," she lied, "so I missed some school. How's it been going?"

"It hasn't."

"What do you mean?" Belle asked.

"A day or two after Mrs. Townsend got killed by lemerons…"

That was wrong. Sash abducted her.

"They shut down the school. Victor said he needed everyone working in their specialty for some reason," Mitch continued. "It was weird. Like he didn't want us to learn anymore, just work."

"Yeah, weird," Belle said.

That sounded like Victor, though. He was obsessed with turning people he didn't like or those who threatened his agenda into dociles. They were the very definition of brainless workers. It made sense he would try to achieve the same goal without actually processing anyone.

Alan Thompson stood at the podium. He was Jack's friend and helped haul off Victor.

"Hello everyone." He cleared his throat into his hand. "I'm rattled like the rest of you. You think you know someone," he shook his head, "then they turn out to be destroying the community you love. Victor betrayed us all. I'll never forget it. But I also won't forget who stood up for what's right: Jack Caraway. I nominate him as interim elder in place of Victor."

Alan stepped back from the podium, gesturing with an outstretched hand to the back of the room.

Mr. Caraway caught Belle's eye as he approached the platform, much like Isaac had earlier that day. People whispered as he went by. He stood on the podium and addressed the assembled crowd.

"There have always been two elders leading the Commune since our founding two hundred years ago. I stand before you as a fellow member of this community. Presently we only have one interim elder leading us. Today, I'm here to stand as the second. According to our founders, there must always be two."

The crowd murmured as they considered their new candidate.

"But it won't be you," Isaac said, walking down the aisle to the podium.

Belle's face darkened. He was wearing black pants, like the pant leg she glimpsed in the school. Was he trying to stop this assembly?

Isaac stood in front of the platform and addressed the room. He could have climbed the platform and taken over the podium. But no. He remained on the same level as everyone else. This was a ploy to show the people he was one of them.

"Sneaky," she said under her breath.

"What?" Mitch asked.

"Nothing. Nevermind."

Isaac was sharper than she thought.

"This man had his friend nominate him after hauling Victor away to a cell. Need I remind you that both Jack and the man nominating him deposed Victor? When no one else stood against our fallen elder, he was the first. Only then did some of you follow. By removing Victor from power himself, he hoped to gain your confidence. He postured as though he were protecting you. He acted strategically to try to seize power for himself."

"That's not true," Jack gripped the sides of the podium. "The evidence of Victor's deceit is at the wall. You all know he did us no service by luring those monsters to our home.

They will destroy everything and everyone we love. We're stronger if we work together. I am up here today to work with you and for you as an interim elder."

Isaac clapped slowly, sarcastically.

"Very well said. Only I believe you're just echoing my words. If you can't make a case for yourself with your own words, how would you be as a leader? Mimicking me the entire time? I'm sacrificing my interests to lead our people through this threat. You are only seeking to advance your own."

Belle's face burned hot. Isaac was projecting all of his behavior onto Mr. Caraway.

Jack opened his mouth to speak, but Isaac held up his hands.

"I call for a vote. If you are for this man say 'aye,' if you oppose say 'nay.'"

The room erupted at once with a garbled response. Belle tried to make out the distinct responses, but it was too loud to tell.

Mitch called out, "nay."

Her stomach plummeted. How could her classmate be so blind?

Isaac raised his hands, similar to how Victor would to call for silence.

"Thank you all for casting your votes. It is clear to me, and everyone here, that the majority of you said 'nay.'" He turned to Jennie's father. "Thank you for your efforts, Mr. Caraway, but the good people have spoken. You will not be an elder."

Jack's face reddened. He stomped down the steps, across the room, and out the door. They failed.

TWENTY-THREE

Ethan
———————

S leep helped his tired body, but his heart was still broken. No amount of rest could heal that.

Ethan stared at the ceiling above him. The thatched roof was a welcome sight. It was nice to be in a treehouse again, only he wished he was in his own home.

When he knocked on Tulsi's door the night before, she opened it. She jumped into his arms, gripping him tight. Her raven black hair was neatly combed and straight as one of his arrows. It flowed like silk over her shoulders.

"Ethan, I thought you were dead!" she said. "Of course, you can stay here."

She gave Jennie a curious look, then raised her eyebrows at him. "Who is this, and what in the world happened out there?"

"This is Jennie." He squeezed Jennie's hand. She shied behind him.

"I can see you two have been through a lot. You can fill me in tomorrow after you've had some rest." She stepped inside, letting them in.

Tulsi's house was tiny, and situated towards the edge of Arborville. It was one of the newer homes. She was a couple years older than Ethan and wanted to move out on her own. People usually did that around here when they turned twenty.

She hadn't decorated it much. There was a little wooden table, a chair, a kitchenette, and a sleeping loft.

"I just have to ask, why come here and not to your house?" Tulsi opened a tall cabinet and took out a couple blankets.

"I can't go back there," Ethan grumbled.

Tulsi hugged the blankets to her chest, studying him. "Right. We can talk about it later… only if you want, though. You can stay here, but the loft only sleeps one," she held out the blankets, giving them an apologetic look. "Sorry, I don't have anything more comfortable than the floor."

"Trust me," Ethan said, "it's an improvement from where we have been sleeping. It's better than the lemeron infested ground."

Thanks to my father, I can't stand to sleep in the same house as him. I had been looking forward to sleeping on my plush stuffed mat.

His father. Just thinking those words soured his mind. He let Ethan believe he adopted him, but he was his biological father. The lie hurt more than the truth.

Why couldn't he have made something else up, like he really was his father and his mother died? Would that lie have hurt any less?

When morning broke, Ethan sat up. Jennie was still sound asleep beside him. Her deep breathing was calming. He wished he could have slept that well last night. He tossed and turned, reliving the night before.

He took the photo he once cherished out of his pocket. Unfolding it, he looked at the face of his mother, Marlene. She hadn't aged at all since the day this photo was taken eighteen years ago. On her lap, she held Ethan as a baby.

He turned the picture over and read the note she'd written on the back.

My dearest son Ethan,

You have brought me so much happiness in your short life, and I wish our time together could have been longer. The world in which we live is no longer safe, and I am unable to keep you from the growing dangers....

His hands shook. The faded ink blurred as tears welled in his eyes. *I've had enough of her lies... and my father's.*

She didn't leave him to try and keep him safe. She was selfish and didn't want the responsibility of being a mother. That much was clear based on how cold she had been.

Her attitude when she told Ethan about his father was 'get over it.' She didn't know what it was like. Marlene abandoned him. Brenden lied to him. Ethan couldn't even think of them as his mother and father anymore.

He had enough of the lies. He had enough of them.

Turning the worn paper over, he looked at the image one last time. His mother's face stared at him. Telling him again to just get over it.

No, she can get over it herself. I'm done with my parents. I don't need them.

He gripped the top edge of the picture and tore it down the middle. Putting the two strips together, he turned them sideways and ripped it in half again. And again. And again. His fingers trembled as he let the pieces fall to the floor.

That photo was the only thing he'd had his entire life. Now he destroyed it. A pang of regret stabbed his heart.

What have I done? He buried his face in his hands. *What am I doing? I don't know anymore. I don't know anything anymore.*

"Ethan?" Tulsi asked.

He lowered his hands. They came away wet with tears. He looked down at Jennie, sleeping on the floor beside him. At least she wouldn't see him crying.

"Ethan, what's wrong?"

He looked up to see Tulsi standing beside the ladder to the sleeping loft. His face burned hot from embarrassment. How much had she seen?

"I just need some air," he climbed to his feet and went to the door, drying his face on his sleeve.

Outside, the morning air was crisp and cool. He leaned over the platform rail. Everything had a purplish hue as the sun broke the horizon.

Purple, like my door.

He clenched his fist. He couldn't even see a color without thinking of the place he used to call home, and all the lies that went with it.

Tulsi leaned over the rail next to him.

"Did she do something to upset you?"

The question startled Ethan.

"Who? Jennie? No. She would never."

"Then why are you so upset?" Tulsi asked.

He shook his head. "I don't want to talk about it."

She took a step back so she could face him directly. Her big brown eyes darted over his face, trying to read him.

"I'm your best friend, you can tell me anything. Ethan, what's wrong? I'm worried about you. You disappear for days on end and come back different... and with a girl, too. What happened to you out there? I've never seen you like this."

"It's just-" Ethan sighed. He didn't know how to explain what he was feeling. "It's just that I found out that my adoptive father is *actually* my father."

Tulsi scrunched up her face. "You mean he didn't just find you in the woods? It was all planned somehow?"

"It seems that way."

"Well, that's a good thing, isn't it?" She asked.

"Being lied to my whole life? How is that a good thing? Just leave it alone, please." Ethan snapped. He groaned. Tulsi didn't deserve that. "I'm sorry. It's just, my whole life has been a lie. I… I don't know…" He trailed off.

"Who told you about your father?" Tulsi glanced over at the door.

Ethan leaned on the railing, looking at the purplish ground below. It was turning pink as the day brightened.

"My mother."

"Your *mother*?" Tulsi shrieked. "Where is she? Is she here?"

"She is now, but I first saw her in the Commune."

Tulsi shook her head, confused. "What's the Commune?"

"It's a whole town of people living in the middle of the forest. There's a huge wall surrounding it to keep them safe. That's where Jennie's from… and my mother."

She narrowed her eyes at Ethan. "They're from the same place? It sounds to me like Jennie had more to do with this than you're willing to admit."

Ethan shook his head. "No, she was only trying to help."

"Help with what?" She crossed her arms and jutted out her hip. "Really, Ethan, I'm worried for you. I've never seen you this upset. She had a hand in this. Trying to help or not, she ended up scrambling your life worse than an egg."

He couldn't help smirking. Tulsi always had a way with colorful analogies.

"You're right about one thing, my life's a mess right now. But Jennie's not the reason for that. She's one of the few good things to ever happen to me."

Tulsi dropped her arms to her side. "If you feel that way, then I'm happy for you. Only, it breaks my heart that you lost your identity in the process."

Ethan shoved off the rail to face her. "How dare you? I

found out who I really was when I met Jennie. I didn't lose a shred of who I am."

"Are you still Ethan *McAllister*?"

He scoffed. "Yes."

"Isn't that your father's last name, though?"

"Well, yeah. It's my last name, too. Why should I give it up?"

She gave him a wry smile. "You shouldn't. Because you're Brenden's son. By name. By blood," she shrugged. "It doesn't matter how. You're still his son."

Ethan opened his mouth to speak, but he didn't know what to say. Tulsi twisted it all around to where it seemed right. Maybe she had a point? His father *had* raised him. It didn't excuse the lies, though. A lifetime of lies. How could he forgive that?

TWENTY-FOUR

Jennie

_____

The house was quiet when Jennie woke. Stretching out her arms across the floor felt good. It was smooth, unlike the rough ground. Sleeping with rocks and roots jabbing in her back was not something she enjoyed. Spending the night on the floor wasn't either, but it was a marked improvement.

She brought her arms back down to her sides. Her fingers stroked the soft woolen blanket. It was nice to have such a luxurious covering to keep her warm. Even back at the Commune, her bedcover wasn't this nice. Or this thick.

I wonder where they get the wool.

They grew cotton in one of the fields back home. Only so much could be produced every year, so new clothing, bedding, and linens were heavily rationed. As a result, her bedding was covered in threadbare patches.

Smiling, she bunched the wool blanket up in her fists. It must be a finger-width thick.

"Ahhh," she sighed.

Despite all the problems plaguing her, her people, and Ethan, that was the best sleep she had in a long time.

The house was silent. Finally opening her eyes, she looked

around. Ethan's blanket was sprawled out on the floor beside her, but he was gone.

Something scattered on the floor next to the fleece caught her eye. She crawled over to it and gasped.

"Oh no," her heart ached for Ethan. "What did you do?"

Back at the Commune, Ethan showed her the picture of his mother with the letter on the back. She remembered how Marlene's eyes and Ethan's were the same green. Now it lay in tatters on the floor.

She turned all the little torn bits of paper over, so the faded color side was up. One square at a time, she pieced Marlene and Ethan back together. First, Marlene's face. Then her hair, his face, his smile... oh, how she wished he would smile like that again... Marlene's hands. Her fingers lovingly holding Ethan upright.

Jennie shook her head. There was so much love in this picture. Where did it all go? The world was cruel to divide such a happy family. Now, they were torn apart, just like this fractured image.

"Just leave it alone," Ethan shouted from outside.

She leapt to her feet. Marlene or his father must have tracked him down. They couldn't even let him have a day to cool down. If they were out there, she wasn't going to let him face them alone.

"Ethan has every right to be upset with you right now," she practiced saying out loud. "Give him his space."

No. That was what Marlene was planning on doing... indefinitely. She was so willing to sever ties with any relationship as if it were an inconvenience.

"You need to make an effort to make things right with your son. The son you abandoned."

There. That was better.

She could rehearse all day, but that wouldn't help Ethan. It was better to be by his side than pacing in here, talking to the walls.

Jennie threw the door open.

"Ethan has ev-" she stopped abruptly.

Where was Marlene? Brenden?

They weren't there. Only Ethan and Tulsi who raised one of her arched eyebrows at her.

"I thought I heard arguing. Is Marlene out here?"

"No, it's just us," Ethan said.

"I find it interesting that when you hear conflict, you think it's one of your own. That says a lot about you people."

She recoiled at Tulsi's remark. It wasn't fair to lump everyone in the same bale of hay. Jennie was nothing like Marlene. In fact, very few people were.

"Marlene is nothing like the rest of us," she crossed her arms. "No offense to Ethan, but she's a recluse and a bit selfish."

"Then why did you bring her here?"

Ethan cleared his throat. "Actually, we were trying to catch up to her."

"Why was she coming here then? To find you?"

"Partly..."

Tulsi rolled her eyes. "Stop beating around the bush. Spit it out."

"She was on her way here to ask us for help."

Her brow pinched together, creating a deep vertical line above her pointed nose. "Why would she need our help?"

"Because the lemerons are swarming at our wall," Jennie said.

Tulsi's face went slack. A little light went on in her eyes as though all the pieces to this puzzle finally clicked in place.

"Holy tree leaves. The lemeron migration. That's what you went to investigate. They've been heading to Jennie's settlement this whole time." She swallowed. "How many are there?"

Ethan blew out a long breath of air. "Hundreds and more coming. The Commune is in great danger. We need to help if we can." He took Jennie's hands. "I'm sorry, Jennie. I lost sight of the bigger problem. We need to save your home. My meager problems aren't important next to this."

Jennie stepped closer to him. She could smell the forest on him. "It's all important. The wall will hold together for a few more days, but your family may not. Please talk to your parents again."

He dropped her hands, shoving away from her. The scowl on his face cut through her heart. Her jaw trembled.

What did I say?

"I can't forgive them. Ever. Neither of you can change my mind. If you're not going to support me in this, then I need to be on my own."

Jennie bit her lower lip, breaking the cut on it open again. The autumn leaves blurred together through her tears, looking like the forest caught fire. Just last night, Ethan wanted to run away with her. Now, he was leaving Jennie alone in this hell.

TWENTY-FIVE

Marlene

"Damn drama," Marlene plopped into a chair by the fire.

"What's that?" Brenden asked, stoking the glowing logs.

Marlene let out a heavy sigh. Her head was pounding from lack of sleep. All night she tossed and turned, thinking about the mess she'd made.

"I spent the last eighteen years worrying about Ethan. Now he wants nothing to do with me." She rubbed her temples. "I missed you as much as him. When I saw you, I couldn't help myself, I had to embrace you again."

He took her hand and kissed it. "Eighteen years is a long time."

"Someday Ethan will understand." She stroked his dark brown hair salted with grey. "Do you think he'll get past this?"

"In time. The boy's got a bit of your fierceness."

"I'm not sure that's a good thing. He hates me. I saw it in his eyes."

Brenden added another log onto the fire. It threatened to smother the flames, but he poked it with a metal rod. The flames came to life again, stronger than ever. A bead of sweat formed on his brow. "He's not happy with me either, but he'll work through it. I'm not ready to give up on him."

His arms were more muscular than she remembered, and the cut of his torso left her longing for him. All of him. The long years apart made him more attractive than ever.

"I should have left the Commune the day I gave you Ethan. We could have been happy out here together." She clenched her fist. "Why didn't I just leave it all behind?"

"I still remember the last time we met when you placed Ethan in my arms. It was in our clearing in the forest, the one with the wild strawberries," Brenden said. "Do you remember what you said to me?"

Marlene nodded. "I said, 'You need to safeguard our son, things are getting too dangerous in the Commune. I need to protect my people, and I can't do that until I root out every malicious person in the Order. Only then can I rejoin you.'"

She slumped her shoulders. "I lost sight of everything. I spent so much time working in the shadows, thinking I just needed more time. Before I knew it, too many years passed, and I failed to make progress." Her lower lip trembled. "I gave up."

Brenden squeezed her hand. "Every month, I went back to the clearing and waited for you, but you never showed. I thought you would return to me, but maybe you just needed a little more time." He lowered his head. "I'm ashamed to admit, I gave up, too. I stopped going to the clearing to wait. I couldn't spend my days sitting around for someone who would never show. I had Ethan to look after. He needed to be my priority."

Marlene's heart shattered in her chest. "I'm sorry," she choked out. "I've let down the most important people to me."

"Ethan's right, you know. I should have told him the truth." Brenden bowed his head. "The lie was easier to live with. It would've been too hard to tell him about you. It hurt less to pretend I didn't know who you were."

Marlene frowned. "Why?"

"Because I missed you too much. Each morning, I woke up another day older and emptier inside. It was easier for me if Ethan didn't ask about you. If he knew that you and I were his parents, he would have asked me endless questions about who his mother was. How could I tell him about you when it killed me to think of the life we never had together? It was selfish of me. He had a right to know."

Her husband's words tugged at her heart. She suffered in her own way for all these years; she failed to consider how much their separation would hurt both Brenden and Ethan.

"What's done is done," she said. "We both did what we thought was best. Were we wrong? Maybe. But all we can do now is try to make it better."

"Do you think Ethan will ever forgive us?" Brenden asked.

Marlene stared into the orange flames. She wished she could say yes, but honestly, she didn't know. Ethan was proving to be very stubborn, just like her. That was definitely not something in their favor.

A horn blared outside, echoed by another horn. And another.

Marlene sat forward in her chair. "What's going on?"

Brenden leapt up. He retrieved two bows and two quivers full of arrows, then rushed to the door.

"Brenden, answer me. What's happening?"

He paused with his hand on the handle. He gave her a longing look with those deep brown eyes.

"Lemerons. Stay here, where it's safe."

Marlene's face darkened. She had lost love once before at the hands of the lemerons. It wouldn't happen again.

"Like hell," she snatched her curved sickle blade, following Brenden out the door.

TWENTY-SIX

Jennie

J ennie was sitting outside Tulsi's house, letting her feet dangle over the deck. It was considerate of Tulsi to give her some space to think. She got the feeling Ethan's best friend wasn't too fond of her. She probably just needed time to get to know Jennie better.

She was wondering where Ethan went to cool off when she heard the horn blast from a few trees away. Another sounded a little further off. Soon, a chorus of horns was blaring from all around. It was an ominous siren call in the middle of the woods.

Tulsi flung her door open. "We need to move. Now."

The urgency in her voice pulled Jennie to her feet. Her chest tightened when she saw the bow strung over Tulsi's back.

"What's happening? Why are they blowing the horns?"

"Lemerons," Tulsi said, leading her over a bridge.

Jennie swallowed hard. Maybe it was a false alarm. But the churning in her gut and the intensity in the air told her otherwise.

The lemerons ruled this world with mindless bloodlust. At

the rate they were gathering at the wall, there was sure to be more than just a handful in Arborville.

"Where are we going?" Jennie asked, stumbling across a wobbly bridge.

"I'm taking you to Ethan's house."

"What's wrong with your home?"

"It's too close to the settlement's edge. You'll be safer back at Ethan's house. It's more central and better protected." Tulsi darted up to a scouting platform.

"Chaz, where's Ethan?"

He was busy taking buckets of arrows out of a large chest in the middle of the platform. Placing them around the perimeter, he looked up.

"Haven't seen him," the sentry eyed Jennie with concern. "I remember you. Ethan brought you back. You shouldn't be out here right now, it's not safe." He went back to his work. "Tulsi, get her out of here."

"Let's go."

Jennie trailed unsteadily after her. The bridges bounced as they ran over them. Some were so narrow that when others rushed past them, she had to turn sideways.

The horns blared again.

"We're running out of time."

Jennie scanned the forest floor. She couldn't see any lemerons. Maybe there was only one or two.

"There! I see Ethan." Tulsi broke into a run.

It was hard to keep up on the unstable wood planks. Her heart raced as she chased after Tulsi. Ethan was two trees over.

Her face flushed. He was still here.

Brenden saw Ethan, too, and rushed up behind him. Jennie and Tulsi reached him at the same time as his father.

"Tulsi, Jennie, I need to get by," Ethan said. "I need my weapon."

"Here, son." Brenden unshouldered a bow and extended it to him.

Ethan stared at the offered weapon with narrowed eyes. He looked from the bow to his father, back to the bow. The muscles in Ethan's stubbled jaw rippled. He was grinding his teeth. The horns blared again.

Ethan snatched the bow from his father's hands and slung it over his shoulder. He took a quiver of arrows without a word to Brenden.

"I'll take it from here, Tulsi," Ethan said. "Thanks for helping Jennie."

He pushed past his father, pulling Jennie behind him by the hand. His hand was warm and comforting in hers.

They came to a familiar treehouse that Jennie recognized as Ethan's home. He pushed open the door and escorted her inside.

He dropped the bow and quiver on a nearby chair. Turning back around, he rushed up to Jennie, cupping her face in his hands. She gasped as he pulled her to him and kissed her.

His stubble scratched her face, but his lips were soft and inviting. She relaxed into him.

One of his hands moved behind her head, his fingers interlacing through her auburn hair. His other hand slid down her body until it stopped at the small of her back. Ethan pulled her closer, his muscular arms flexing.

Jennie wrapped her arms around his neck. She closed her eyes, enjoying the moment.

The horns sounded outside.

Ethan broke off the kiss and rested his forehead against hers.

"You're everything to me," he whispered.

Butterflies swarmed in Jennie's stomach, and her body tingled all over.

"I'm sorry for the way I reacted this morning," he said. "I

was wrong to take my frustrations out on you and Tulsi. I overreacted. Please forgive me."

Jennie shook her head, their foreheads still touching. "There's nothing to forgive. You were right to be upset. I'm sorry for everything that's happened since we got here." Jennie released her hold on Ethan and looked him in the eye.

The chorus of horns played their warning song, yet again. "I need to get out there to help," Ethan picked up his bow and quiver. "Stay here, and stay safe."

TWENTY-SEVEN

Ethan

E than jogged to the nearest sentry post, the bridges trembling beneath his feet. Seeing Chester up ahead, he quickened his pace.

Chester brought the signal horn to his lips, blowing the alarm once more.

"Did you spot it?" Ethan asked after Chester lowered the horn.

"No. Not yet. The first signal came from the north," He leaned over the deck railing, scanning the ground below. "But I reckon it'll be coming this way soon."

Ethan glanced around. Usually, the trees would be swarming with hunters and scouts after a signal blast. Only a few others were taking their positions nearby.

"There's too few of us here. Where's everyone else?" Ethan asked.

"Dunno, but something doesn't feel right in the air. It's too still."

Ethan sniffed. "And too rancid. They're coming."

Chester's eyes went wide. "You mean there's more than one?"

Ethan nodded. "And I know where they're going."

Arborville wouldn't be their destination. It would be the Commune. Maybe if they could destroy these lemerons, it would help ease the burden on Jennie's people.

He readied his bow with an arrow. The ground was still. Not even a breeze rustled the leaves blanketing the forest floor.

And then he heard it. Lemerons growled just beyond his sightline. The trees provided his people protection, but they also obstructed his view. A bowstring snapped and a lemeron roared.

Men and women shouted commands at each other, tension breaking through their voices.

Chester ran a hand through his shaggy hair. "How many are there?"

"It doesn't matter, even one is too many."

Ethan saw movement below. He steadied his aim and loosed an arrow sending it through the trees to find its mark. The creature let out a gargled cry before collapsing motionless to the ground.

"One less to worry about." Ethan readied another arrow.

Chester hooked the horn on his belt and picked up a crossbow. He fit it with a bolt and cranked the arming mechanism.

"Save your shots until they get closer," Ethan warned.

Crossbows were deadly, but not as accurate at a distance. He preferred a bow and arrow over a crossbow any day.

Another lemeron stepped into view. This time, his arrow caught its shoulder. It staggered back, roared, then rushed forward in a frenzy. Its head bobbed wildly as it clawed at anything in its path.

Ethan loosed another arrow. It zipped right past the lemeron's head, missing.

"Damn it!"

Chester stepped beside him, taking aim with the crossbow. The lemeron was nearly beneath them. He squeezed the trigger.

The bolt bit into the lemerons chest, right where the heart would be. It staggered back, then advanced a few more steps before collapsing. It was dead.

Ethan clapped him on the back.

"Nice shot."

His smile fell when he saw his father running into view a few trees away. Their eyes met.

"Ethan," he shouted. "We need you over here. There's too many of them."

He drew in a sharp breath. Shouldering his bow, he ran.

Ethan sprinted over the bridges and up the steps to the upper level of treehouses. His father gripped his shoulder.

"We need your help. We're being overrun,"

"How?" Ethan asked.

His father's hand tightened on his shoulder, his voice strained as he spoke. "They're starting to climb."

Ethan's stomach clenched. "What? That's impossible. They can't, they don't know how."

"Look down, they're learning."

Ethan swallowed his fear and peered at the battle below.

On the level beneath them, he saw his people attacking. Men and women alike were firing arrows, bolts, and dropping huge stones on the creatures swarming the ground. There must have been at least three dozen lemerons. So, this was where everyone was, over here fighting the vile creatures.

His people were killing them off. As the motionless ones fell, the false life driving them finally extinguished, the others stepped on their corpses. A mound of dead lemerons had formed at the base of a tree. The living ones climbed onto the pile of their dead. The more that died, the higher the rest climbed.

"Impossible," Ethan whispered.

Tulsi was on the lower level, fighting them off as they

ascended. She stood out in her blue shirt, like a bluebird amongst the sparrows. The quiver on her back was empty.

A lemeron climbed so high, it reached across the platform, snatching at her feet. She hurled a heavy stone as big as her head at it. It cracked against the creature's face. It slid off the platform.

Another lemeron quickly replaced it, snarling and clawing at the wood by her feet. She backed away, her back against the treehouse. Ethan's body went numb. There was nowhere for her to go. She was sandwiched in by other scouts fighting them off. And even worse, she was out of arrows and rocks.

Ethan's eyes darted around, searching for the quickest path to her. The lemeron grabbed her ankle and pulled. She fell down with a shriek.

There was no time. He fumbled with an arrow, drew back his bowstring, and released it. He leaned over the railing of his high perch, hoping he didn't miss. His arrow soared through the air. Time slowed around him as he begged for the tip to hit its mark.

The lemeron pulled her to the edge, closer to the frenzied mass of creatures below. He held his breath. What if he missed? What if he hit her? His arms trembled.

A wet crack split the air as his arrow sunk into its eye socket. The lemeron went limp with the wooden shaft sticking out of its face.

Tulsi scrambled back from the edge as more lemerons began to climb.

"If they get up there, it's over for us all," his father shouted.

Ethan thought of Jennie, defenseless in his house, and Tulsi, who was nearly pulled down into the waiting hands of death.

"What's your plan?" he asked.

His father thrust the hilt of a short sword in his hand. "We go down there and draw them away."

Ethan stared deep into the eyes of his father. He meant the ground. They might be killed down there, but it would mean the others would have a chance to live. He nodded.

His father returned the gesture, then pulled him into a tight hug. Ethan hugged him back.

"My son," he whispered. "I'm sorry for the lies. I did it for love of your mother. It was too hard for me to speak about her and it was easier to pretend I didn't know her. I couldn't bear talking about your mother knowing I'd probably never see her again. It was selfish of me. I should have told you."

Brenden pulled away, tears in his eyes. The pain and torment his father had suppressed for Ethan's entire life was written plainly across his father's face.

"I forgive you," Ethan heard himself say. He hadn't realized he said the words aloud. It felt good to say it, like a heavy weight was lifted off his chest.

A smile broke through the sadness on his father's face. "Thank you, my son. Now let's go save Arborville."

TWENTY-EIGHT

Marlene

S ince when could lemerons climb? If they used their dead as stepping stones to reach higher ground, how soon until they learned to climb trees... or the wall?

Marlene witnessed a girl nearly get pulled off the deck by a lemeron. That was too close. She probably picked the worst place to be when the creatures learned how to climb: one of the lowest treehouses to the ground.

A well-timed arrow saved her, but another lemeron was climbing onto the platform. Its torso was flat on the wooden surface, all it needed to do was get a leg up, and it was over.

The others fighting next to her let her pass by, and she retreated to higher ground. One of them stabbed the lemeron with his blade. They had it under control for now, but more were climbing.

Marlene was making her way to them to help. On her way, she threw small boulders at the stragglers, picking them off one by one. She was nearly there when something moved at the edge of her sight. It was quick and purposeful... very different from a lemeron.

She turned and gasped. Down on the ground, Brenden and Ethan ran past the pile of lemerons.

"No," she said breathlessly. Her head was buzzing.

Marlene grabbed hold of the railing in front of her, leaning over to get a better look. Her heart hammered in her chest. They were deliberately putting themselves in danger. Why? As one lemeron after another took notice of them, she figured it out. They were luring them away from the pile of dead monsters.

Sniffing out easier prey, the lemerons abandoned their climb and pursued Brenden and Ethan. There was no sense to the direction they ran in. They circled trees, ducked under branches, and, most importantly, confused the creatures.

One of the monsters stopped in its tracks, bobbing its head around, trying to figure out where its prey went. Ethan ran in front of it, pulling its gaze. Brenden rushed at it from behind, plunging a blade through its back.

Brown blood exploded from the wound. It collapsed to the ground, dead.

Without missing a beat, Brenden took off. This time he distracted a lemeron, giving Ethan a chance to cut its head off with his sword. Marlene raised an eyebrow. A blow like that took enormous strength and precision.

She watched in admiration as her husband and son continued to pick off the monsters. The way they moved and attacked was practiced and well thought out. They were in sync with each other. The grey fleshed beasts were no match for the two men.

Movement caught her eye. From the woods, a group of five more lemerons approached. Fast. Brenden and Ethan continued their dance, killing the lemerons who abandoned the pile.

"Look behind you," she shouted, doubtful they could hear her. She was too far away.

Time to act. Gripping the railing, she vaulted over it and dropped to the ground. Marlene landed in a crouch, looking up in time to see a lemeron snap its head toward her. It opened its nasty mouth, letting out a crackled scream as it charged.

She sprung to her feet, drawing her sickle. Slashing the curved blade in front of her, she opened the lemeron's throat. Congealed brown blood splattered her face. She grimaced, wiping her mouth with the back of her hand.

Stepping on its corpse, she dashed through the chaos of battle. Ethan swung wildly, cutting down advancing creatures with his sword in one hand and dagger in another.

Marlene gave a nod of approval as she passed him. A blade in each hand was smart. He blinked, shaking his head, confused. There was no time to stop and explain. A lemeron snarled and lunged at Ethan. Brenden stabbed it through the side.

They were being overrun and still didn't notice the five other monsters running right for them.

She charged past the advancing group, slicing the head off one as she went by. Its head hit the ground with a wet thump. The other four stopped to face her.

These were people once. One still had the tattered remains of a dress hanging limply off bony shoulders. Its slack jaw tightened as it snarled and charged.

Marlene slashed at it, cutting its arm off. The lemeron didn't even notice. It continued attacking, brandishing dirty fingernails and blackened teeth.

As she reached back, preparing to strike a blow, another seized her from behind. The ragged breath it drew rattled in Marlene's ear.

Don't let it bite you!

She squirmed, pulling frantically away from its face as the lemeron opened its mouth.

"Not today," she yelled, twisting her arm free.

She rammed her elbow back, connecting to its jaw with a

wet crack. The monster loosened its grip, giving her enough room to strike. Her blade stabbed the lemeron right through its open mouth. Its limbs went limp and crumpled to the ground.

She charged the one-armed lemeron in the tattered dress, aiming her sickle at its neck.

Marlene roared as she sliced its head clean off. It fell lifeless to the forest floor.

Two more to go.

They charged her at the same time. Marlene crouched. Extending her arm, she adjusted her grip on her sickle. Narrowing her eyes, she waited for them to get closer. When they were almost upon her, she sprung up, spinning in a circle. She felt resistance as her blade made contact two times.

She stopped, her back to the creatures. She glanced over her shoulder in time to see the two headless creatures collapse, dead.

Ethan and Brenden were still fighting off the remaining lemerons. Red blood streamed down the side of Brenden's face. Three of the monsters backed him against a tree as he tried to fight them off. Ethan was busy with two of his own.

Marlene's temper flared. No one - living or dead - threatened her family. She charged, swinging wildly, cutting down anything in her path.

Letting out a shrill scream, she cut and slashed with her sickle. The blade cut air and lemeron flesh alike. It felt good. The sound of flesh ripping open was like music to her. Like the song always calling her. The one that was currently calling her back to the wall. She fought it for so long. It was so loud now, welcoming her to oblivion.

"Marlene. Marlene! Stop!" Brenden screamed.

She froze, blinking. Her arm raised, ready to strike. Only, all the lemerons were dead. Her target was Brenden. Holding his sword protectively in front of him, his eyes were wide and fearful.

"Oh," she gasped.

Marlene staggered back, dropping her sickle. She sank to her knees, trembling. *What's happening to me? I almost killed my husband.*

TWENTY-NINE

Travis

That didn't go as planned. Travis's father should have been the perfect candidate for a stand-in elder. But Isaac twisted his intentions. He made it seem like his father stepped up to remove Victor to clear the position for himself.

It had been nearly a week since Marlene left and there was still no sign of her returning. The stench outside was becoming unbearable. It meant only one thing: more lemerons were reaching the wall.

Travis rubbed his sweaty palms on his pants. He really needed to stop doing that. It was a nervous habit, but he couldn't help it. He balled his hands into fists, hoping that might be better.

His father's angry voice brought his attention back to the meeting. Travis, Jack, and Belle were meeting with Uncle Albert in the back of his shop.

"I've been made a fool of by that snake. I didn't want to get involved in this charade, but you made these two convince me," Jack pointed at the old man. "Your idea didn't work. Isaac outmaneuvered us."

"We'll try with someone else," Uncle Albert said, jotting some numbers down on a piece of parchment.

"Like who, Belle?" His father asked sarcastically.

The old man's wrinkled hand paused. He looked up, peering at her through his thick glasses. Tapping the end of his feather quill to his cheek, he looked thoughtful.

"Excellent idea," he pointed the feather at Belle. "You will stand as a candidate for the interim elder."

She jerked her head back, scoffing. "You've got to be kidding me. There's no chance I'll be elected. Think about the word, el-der," she said, punctuating each syllable. "I'm only seventeen. Over half the Commune's older than me. Pick someone else."

"It has to be you," Uncle Albert said.

"No way. Just this morning, you said it had to be Mr. Caraway. Look how that turned out," she leaned back in her chair and crossed her arms. "I say just let things lie. Marlene will be back soon enough to fix it."

"Will she?" Uncle Albert pursed his lips.

Travis leaned forward. "You think she's not coming back? What about the help she was going to bring with her? What about Jennie?"

The old man set his quill down and stoppered his ink. "I don't know any more than you about the happenings beyond the wall. Depending on them can't be our only choice." He turned to Belle. "We have to take action ourselves, or all of us will perish."

She shook her head. "It's still not going to be me."

Travis's father cleared his throat. "He's right, Belle. You stand the best chance, and we can depend on you to do the right thing."

"Have you all lost your senses? Why on earth would *anyone* vote for a teenager to be their leader?" she protested.

"No one can argue about your motives." Jack leaned in. "They think I'm corrupt and power-hungry because I hauled Victor away, but you don't have any dirt on your hands."

"And I don't have any experience under my belt, either."

"You have more than you realize," Uncle Albert rose. "I think we've all had a long day. Let's get some rest and start fresh in the morning."

Belle got up and left without another word.

"That was awkward," Travis mumbled to himself.

His father patted him on the back. "Come on, let's go home."

They left together, walking in silence down the narrow streets. Their house felt so empty with Jennie gone. Her bed was still neatly made as though she just got up and started her day. But she never came home to sleep under her covers.

"You want a drink?" His father asked.

Travis shrugged. "I guess some water."

His father filled up two glasses of water and placed them on the kitchen table. Travis sat, taking a drink.

Jack rubbed his hand down his face. He looked older than he had in the morning. Wrinkles scratched their worry across his forehead.

"This whole situation's dangerous for all of us. If we take action, we're shut down. If we do nothing, we're still down."

Travis furrowed his brow, not quite understanding what his father meant. "So... what should we do?"

His father took a long drink of water, emptying his glass. He set it on the table with a clang.

"We've done all we can today. Now let's get some sleep and see what tomorrow brings."

THIRTY

Belle

The tolling of the schoolhouse bell interrupted Belle's deep sleep.

"Again?" she grumbled.

She rolled out of bed, irritated she had to leave her warm blankets. This would be the third assembly in two days. Enough was enough.

She got dressed and went to the bathroom. She washed her face, hoping the water would help wake her up. Her bloodshot eyes didn't want to stay open. What she would do for a cup of coffee… but rations were tighter now, and Travis didn't have his kitchen connections anymore.

Since Marlene left, rations were severely limited. Those in charge of provisions imposed restrictions of their own accord. They called it caution. Belle called it panic.

She left the bathroom and walked into the main living room where her mom reclined on the couch reading a worn book. On the table beside her sat a cup of hot water with several apple slices in it. When rations were tight, her mom liked to pretend it was "tea."

To Belle, it was just a cup of water with an apple in it.

"Are you ready to go?" Her mom asked, looking up from her book.

"Yeah," Belle glanced around. "Where's dad?"

"He's already headed over. I was waiting for you."

"Thanks," she mumbled, trying to rub the sleep from her eyes.

Together she walked with her mom past the rows of houses and the shops. By the time they reached the town square, the bell stopped ringing. People were still pouring into the meeting hall of the Sanctuary.

Everyone was filing in like little worker bees in a beehive. No identity, just drones working to keep the queen alive.

"This is ridiculous," Belle grumbled.

"What's that?" her mom asked.

"Nothing."

"Be careful with that, you don't want people getting the wrong idea," her mom warned in her airy voice.

Belle bit her tongue instead of responding.

Inside, she took her usual seat in the student section at the back. She crossed her arms and waited. People shifted on their benches as gossip and whispers filled the air.

It was definitely an improvement from just the other day when everyone thought everyone else was out to get them. Paranoia did no good for a community. At least Isaac did one thing right.

Belle scoffed. *We'll see how long that lasts.*

The door slammed shut, and the room grew quiet. A pair of shuffling feet swished across the floor. Belle's jaw dropped open when she saw Uncle Albert slowly making his way to the podium. She felt the blood drain from her face. What was he up to?

He never left his shop. Never. Not even for mandatory assemblies.

Everyone was okay with it because he was so old and frail. He was just the friendly apothecary shop owner across

144

the way. He got his updates and news from his customers, so he stayed informed on what went on during meetings.

He climbed the steps to the podium on shaky legs. When he settled in at the top, he cleared his throat. His voice was scratchy as he addressed the room.

"Hello, my dear friends and neighbors. It's been years since I left my shop to come to an assembly. These old bones don't let me get very far."

A few people chuckled sympathetically.

"I know that we have unwanted visitors outside, and we're missing an elder. I'm concerned for us all, but I'm thankful to Isaac here," he gestured to Isaac sitting off to the side of the podium, "for volunteering to help us as interim elder."

Some people in the room clapped. Isaac shined a forced smile and nodded at Albert.

"It's such a burden for one person to bear, so I would like to offer up the name of someone I think can help."

Belle sat up, straight as a stick.

Oh no, he's not really going to do this.

"This is someone I believe in. She is smart, skilled, and concerned for our safety."

No, no, no. Belle swallowed her protest.

"I know she will be a wonderful help to Isaac and all of us until Elder Marlene comes back. With that said, I would like to propose Belle Joiner serve as interim elder."

No! Why would he do this? She told him she wouldn't. He was forcing her into it in the most public way possible. She tried to shrink into a little ball so she could disappear.

Isaac cleared his throat and stood. "Thank you, dear friend, for your thoughtful proposal."

Yeah, right. They aren't friends. Isaac just probably doesn't know his name.

"All in favor, say aye," Isaac said.

To her surprise, many of the people in the room gave their

consent. Did they just not realize she was a teenager trying to play with the big kids?

"All opposed say nay."

Only a few people in the room said nay. They were probably members of the Order who only wanted their own in power.

"The ayes have it," Isaac announced, his smile faltering. "Would our newest elder, Belle Joiner, please join us on the podium?"

She stood on rubber legs. She stuffed her hands in her pockets, so no one could see them shaking. She abandoned her chair and walked down the aisle. Every single eye in the room was on her. She felt them all, from curious glances to hateful stares.

When she reached the top of the platform, someone started clapping. Others joined in. Soon, the room was filled with people clapping just for her.

She swallowed, hoping she wouldn't have to make a speech.

Managing something, she said, "thank you for this opportunity to help."

Isaac shook her hand in front of the crowd as if congratulating her. He grinned at Belle, but his eyes said, "watch your back."

THIRTY-ONE

Sash

S ash trekked down the long corridor. Bare lightbulbs suspended from the ceiling cast light every few yards. The thick, blue glass provided the only separation between him and his victims. As he walked, he felt their eyes on him. They cowered in the back of their concrete cells.

He wondered if they remembered who he was. A docile couldn't talk back, which is what he liked about them. They also couldn't conspire, unlike those filthy undesirables.

He huffed. He showed them, though. Each resident in a cell was an undesirable who the Order took down. Sash relished walking through the corridor containing his trophies. His chest swelled as he went further in.

Each of these dull creatures was a person he obtained and brought to Goggles. They achieved their higher calling by successfully undergoing processing. Those that failed the transformation died and were put in the morgue drawers in the lab. It didn't matter much to Sash. Either way, he eliminated a target and furthered the Order's initiative.

He stopped outside of the last inhabited cell. There were plenty more vacant ones on ahead, just waiting to be filled.

Only a matter of time, he thought.

He rapped on the blue glass, the crack of it echoing through the dim hall. A groan answered from within.

Victor, or what was left of him, stepped into the edge of the light. His face was sunken in, more gaunt than ever. The transformation was taking hold.

A yellow film crept into the edges of his eyes. Sash could still see intelligence behind Victor's eyes, but soon that would fade - just like the rest of him. He would become another mindless creature.

Victor's haggard face contorted into a mixed expression of anger, fear, and begging. He opened his mouth as if to speak, but only a hoarse groan came out.

"Save your breath," Sash sneered. "You earned this. You used me as a tool. I've got a new ally now. Someone who sees my true worth."

Victor lifted a weak arm, placing his hand on the blue glass partition. He widened his cloudy eyes, groaning.

Sash curled his lip. "You really are disgusting. Enjoy your new purpose of serving others."

After turning to go back the way he came, he froze, his heart pausing in his chest.

Every docile he passed by earlier stood so close to the glass, they almost touched it. They never did that. They always cowered in the back of their cells where it's dark.

Their bodies were rigid as a wooden board. They didn't move, but all of them were staring at him.

He trudged forward. Each docile's gaze fixated on him. As he passed by, only their heads moved, keeping their yellow eyes locked on him. He quickened his pace, rushing back to the processing lab at the end of the hall. But the faster he went, the faster their creepy heads turned.

He was nearly running now. The hammering of his feet on the concrete floor echoed through the hall. Yellow orbs flickered as he ran past. Their eyes still followed him.

Finally, he reached the door. He flung it open, rushing

inside. Slamming it shut, he locked it behind him. He pushed off the door and crossed the lab to the little office.

Goggles looked up from his papers, startled from the intrusion.

"What have you been feeding those things?" Sash grunted. Somehow this was the scrawny scientist's fault.

"Nothing lately. They won't require sustenance for another few weeks." He cocked his head to the side. "Why?"

Sash pointed at the door to the cells. "Those things in there are acting weird."

Goggles drew in a quick breath. "In what way? Tell me everything."

"It was like all of them were acting together. They were staring me down. *Me.* I delivered them here for a better life, and they glare at me with those damn yellow eyes."

Goggles snatched a piece of paper and pencil, scribbling furiously as Sash spoke. He mumbled something about intent as he wrote.

"I've had enough of this place," Sash tossed up his hands in exasperation. "I'm going up to finally get some fresh air and fresh victims."

"Perfect," a voice behind him said.

Sash spun around.

"Isaac!"

How long had he been standing there? Sash hunched over, feeling ashamed for planning to defy Isaac's request: stay here, protect Goggles.

After he'd been given a chance to be an equal part of the order, he was throwing it away.

Wait... Isaac said, "perfect." Does he want me to return to the surface?

"There's been a development that I need you to take care of," Isaac said.

"What is it?"

"I've located your curly-haired girl. She'll be easy to find now that she's an elder."

Sash narrowed his eyes, not understanding what he meant.

"Belle Joiner was just elected as the other interim elder," Isaac said. "I tried to track down who rang the bell for the assembly yesterday. I suspect it was her. She snuck out of the school before I could catch her. Belle probably called the assembly today, too, so she could be elected. She needs to be eliminated."

A greedy sneer spread across Sash's face. "I'm on it."

THIRTY-TWO

Jennie

_____

J ennie sat against the wall with her knees tucked to her chest. Covering her ears didn't help suppress the sounds of fighting outside. People shouted, weapons cracked, heavy objects slammed on the ground. But the worst were the horrible sounds coming from the lemerons.

Each time one growled, screeched, or snarled, she thought of her mother. A cold shiver sliced through her from head to toe. Hearing them brought back the vivid memory of her mother being attacked by one in the woods. She remembered clinging to Travis after they fled the forest.

"Did you see?" Jennie asked her little brother, only eight at the time.

"I saw a lemeron," he sobbed.

Jennie's heart raced. He shouldn't see such horrors at his age.

"But did you see what happened?"

He shook his head and whimpered. "Where's mother?"

Jennie closed her eyes and saw the lemeron biting into her mother's creamy flesh. She shuddered, wondering if there was anything left of her.

"She's gone," Jennie cried, squeezing Travis tighter.

She trembled from the memory. Clasping her hands tighter against her ears, she wanted to drown out the lemerons. The sounds of fighting died down. Maybe it was working. She stayed like that for a long time. It felt like hours to her.

Things grew quiet. She lowered her hands and listened. Was it over?

Tentatively, she stood, taking a slow step toward the door. It burst open; she leapt back with a start.

Ethan limped in, supporting his father by the arm. Her heart skipped a beat. They were alive. She rushed forward, wrapping Brenden's other arm around her shoulder. Together they sat him down in a chair by the fire. Blood streamed down his face from a gash on his forehead.

Jennie grabbed a cloth from her bag and pressed it against the wound.

"Keep the pressure on it to stop the bleeding," she instructed his father.

He silently obeyed

"Where's your mo-" Jennie was about to ask when she appeared.

Marlene walked through the open door, her eyes distant and unfocused. All the color had drained from her face. She didn't say a word or even seem to see them in the room. She just went to the ladder and climbed to the sleeping loft above.

Jennie glanced at Ethan, raising her eyebrows.

"Something happened out there. She wasn't herself for a moment."

Jennie frowned. "What does that mean?"

"We were fighting off the lemerons when she came down to help," Ethan began.

"Down?"

"Ah… yes. The lemerons clambered over a pile of their dead. They reached one of our platforms."

"But they can't climb," Jennie interrupted, panic in her voice.

"They can now. But I don't think they know how to climb trees," he gave Jennie a worried look. "Or walls."

She swallowed, understanding the connotation.

"Then what happened?"

"My father and I went to the ground."

Jennie gasped. "What? Why?"

"They were about to climb onto a platform. I shot one to save Tulsi, but they kept climbing. We gave them something else to focus on. We couldn't let them get up to Arborville. We fought them off as best we could." Ethan paused, looking at his father pressing the rag against his wound. "There were so many."

"They could have killed you," Jennie said in a small voice.

Ethan bit his lower lip. "That's when my mother joined our fight. She decimated them. I've never seen *anyone* fight with such speed or strength," he glanced up at the sleeping loft, lowering his voice. "Or with such frenzy. It's like she lost herself. She attacked anything that moved. When all the lemerons were dead, she charged at my father."

"Why would she do that? Did she do that to him?"

"No, but it's like she couldn't see him. We screamed at her to stop, but she kept charging. Finally, she snapped out of it. I don't think she even realized what she was doing. I don't know her all that well, but even I could see she wasn't herself. She was… something else."

Jennie was stunned.

"Marlene can be cold, but she's not a killer," she added silently to herself, *is she?*

Ethan winced as he sat down.

"You're hurt," Jennie scanned him with her eyes, trying to assess his wounds.

Fresh bruises bloomed on his cheek, and his clothes where splattered with brown blood. His pant leg was stained red and torn just above his ankle. She knelt down in front of him, rolling up his pant leg.

His skin was cut, but it was shallow.

"Just a scratch," Jennie said. "Let me clean it up for you, anyway."

"No, I'm fine. But my father's head might need some stitches. Would you mind?" Ethan asked, adding. "You did such a great job on my arm."

She nodded.

"The sink's over there," he pointed to the kitchen area at the back of the little round house.

It had shelves with food, linens, and plates arranged neatly on them. She took a clean towel from the shelf and ran a little water on it.

She returned to Brenden, pulling a chair up beside him. "Let me clean and bandage your cut."

Ethan's father removed the blood-soaked cloth from his head. She dabbed at the gash with the wet towel. When she pulled it back, more blood flowed from his wound.

"You need stitches." She reached into her bag and pulled out her needle and thread. "I hoped I wouldn't need to use this, but I packed it anyway. Better to be prepared than caught without it, right?"

"Smart girl," Brenden said.

Jennie threaded the needle, her hand hovering over Brenden's head. Glancing down, she caught his eye. "Try not to move. This is going to hurt."

"I'm ready," he gripped the armrests with dirty hands.

Jennie pushed the needle through his skin. Brenden tensed, gritting his teeth through the pain. It took eight stitches to close the cut and stop the bleeding.

She wiped her hands clean on the wet towel before grabbing her roll of bandages from her bag. She wrapped a few layers around his head.

"This will help keep it clean."

"Thank you, Jennie. I'm glad Ethan found you."

A smile tugged at the corner of her mouth. It was hard to smile after such horrors just happened. Ethan and Brenden almost died. They were willing to sacrifice themselves for their people.

All she did was cower inside while they fought bravely. What was she willing to sacrifice? Not Ethan. Next time she will fight by his side and not relive the trauma of her mother's death. Today was the second time she shut down from fear. Today was the last time she ever would.

Wincing, Ethan stood, took a towel from the shelf, and walked to the door. "I need to wash up at the bathhouse."

Jennie looked down at the blood clinging beneath her fingernails. "Can I come? I could use some freshening up."

"Grab a towel and follow me."

THIRTY-THREE

Ethan

It was a long walk to the bathhouse. Limping along, it took more time than usual. His leg hurt. His muscles were on fire. He was battered and bruised. The fighting had been so chaotic, he couldn't remember how he got most of his wounds.

Jennie slipped her hand in his. Just her gentle touch helped.

They walked in silence through the heights of Arborville. The people he saw were still in a state of shock. Never in any living memory had the lemerons attacked in such numbers.

Can we survive another attack like this? Pain shot through Ethan's leg as he stepped onto an unsteady bridge. *Can I survive another attack?*

Chester, Chaz, and a few other sentries were piling the dead lemerons on the forest floor in a small clearing near the center of Arborville. A couple hunters stood at the ready with torches. They would burn the bodies. It relieved Ethan that they didn't have any of their own dead to burn.

There were so many of the monsters. Even lying still, they looked menacing. Snarls were frozen on their faces. He half expected them to crawl from the heap and wage another attack. He shuddered.

They should burn them quickly and be done with it. The last thing they needed was to have those horrors lying around beneath their town.

Ethan crossed the bridge that lead into the cliff at the far end of Arborville. It was a vertical formation of rock that jutted perpendicular from the earth. Half a tree height off the ground, the opening to a cavern sunk into the rock face. This was the only way in or out. It was the only solid ground that was safe for them.

His people removed the trees closest to the cliff, so the only way in was to cross the long suspension bridge. They used the cleared land to create a small field for cultivating food. They also kept sheep nearby for wool.

"It's up here," he said.

"In the cave? I thought the bathhouse would be in another treehouse or something."

"Trust me, this is much better than scrubbing with cold water."

They crossed the bridge and entered the dark mouth of the cave. The cave was always the same temperature throughout the year. It was cool in the summer and warm in the winter. And the natural springs within were always hot.

Mounted torches on the walls burned. He saw something gnarled and grey move ahead. He recoiled and gripped his dagger. Stepping near, he relaxed, letting out an exasperated sigh. It was only the flames casting shadows across a stalagmite. His mind was playing tricks on him.

"What a day," he grumbled, rubbing his hand down his face. Everything weighed so heavily on him.

Ethan pulled Jennie to him and brushed her hair over her shoulder. What would he do if he never saw her again? How could he leave her alone in this world?

"I'm sorry," he whispered.

She leaned into him. "For what?"

"Everything. For bringing you here. It's dangerous in the forest." He wrapped his arms around her, burying his face in her hair. She still smelled sweet, like apples. "I'm afraid it will only get worse. I don't know what I'd do if I lost you."

Her body tensed, she pushed away from him.

"If *you* lost *me*? What about me losing you? You almost died today."

"I know, and I'm sorry." He gripped his hair. "I just had to do something. If the lemerons made it up, they would have killed everyone… including you."

She lowered her gaze. "I guess there's never an easy option." Looking up, she met his eye. "What happens now?"

Ethan took Jennie's hands in his. "Let's start by washing this miserable day off. Then we'll figure it out."

Her smile faltered as the action tugged on her cut lip. Leaning in, he kissed her gently on her mouth.

He pointed down a torch-lit path in the cavern. "If you go that way. You'll get to the ladies' bath. Take your time."

Jennie nodded and disappeared deeper into the cave.

Ethan went down another path. As he neared the hot baths, the steam created a curtain, shrouding the cavern in a silky vapor.

He stripped off his clothes, dropping them in a heap on the floor. Dipping his toe into the pool, he felt for the bottom. He stepped in, careful not to slip. The hot water kissed his skin. Fully committing to the bath, he plunged in, dipping his head beneath the water.

Emerging, he ran his fingers through his hair. He waded further into the depths, the surface of the pool lapping against his chin. Relaxation seeped through him as he let the heat of the water numb his pain.

He needed this. He needed to remove himself from anything and everything. His life had been turned on its head only yesterday, and today he faced death and lived. It felt good to fight alongside his father again.

He let out a sigh. Talking about his mother was too painful for his father. Ethan imagined what it would be like being separated from the woman he loved. Being apart from Jennie during the battle today was difficult enough. He worried for her safety.

How could Ethan be so blind to his father's pain? He'd been so distracted by his own, he neglected the emotions of the man who raised him.

And his mother. What had happened to her today? She'd gone mad like a rabid animal. Anger clouded her eyes. She was fighting more like one of the monsters than a human. If she hadn't snapped out of it, he dreaded what might have happened.

Ethan splashed water on his face. He pushed all thoughts from his mind. All he wanted to do was soak in peace. These thoughts did nothing but torment him.

Closing his eyes, he visualized birds fluttering through the trees. Water trickled in a stream, a deer dipped its head down to take a drink. Wind rustled the leaves.

He let his mind drift away. But it always went back to the crazed look in his mother's eyes. What if it happened again? If it did, Ethan would have a tough choice to make: either do nothing and let Marlene kill his father, or step in and save his father by killing his mother.

He hoped he would never have to make that choice.

THIRTY-FOUR

Jennie

E than was right. The steamy water in the cavern spring was much better than washing in a cold tub. Torches gave just enough light to see by. The warm flickering of the flames along the cave wall was comforting. She couldn't see the bottom of the pool but walked into it.

It sloped gently downward, allowing her to wade in with ease. She ducked down until her shoulders were underwater. She never had a bath so soothing or immersive in her life. In her home, all she had was a small tub and a cup to bathe with. This was heavenly.

Jennie felt along the edge of the pool until she found a ledge to sit on. The stony surface was smooth as a horse's summer coat.

She scrubbed at her fingernails with a washrag she found near the front of the cavern. The caked-on patches of dirt and blood came off easily in the steaming water. She scrubbed her arms, washing away the trauma of the past two weeks.

It was strange how normal her life seemed before Mrs. Townsend taught her class forbidden information. Before then, she was just a normal teenage girl getting ready to finish school and embark on her path to adulthood. When she turned eighteen in only a few months, she would be eligible for an elder advisor position.

Now she knew better. She wanted nothing to do with the corrupt elders in the Commune. Victor brought this doom upon them all, and Marlene was stubborn and self-serving. Even with Victor removed, the person who replaced him would probably be just as bad, if the Order had their way.

"I hope Belle was able to do something about that," she muttered as she scrubbed her shoulder.

"Who's Belle?" A voice called out through the mist.

Jennie started dropping her rag in the pool. Sloshing, she grabbed for it beneath the water. Her aching fingers snatched it before it sank into the dark bottom of the spring.

With her rag recovered, she squinted through the mist to see a slender figure approaching. The woman splashed as she dipped into the deeper part of the pool.

She came into view, her long black hair trailed behind her on the surface of the water.

"Tulsi?" Jennie didn't expect anyone else to be here, but she was glad it was at least someone she had met. It was uncomfortable to bathe naked with someone else, but even more awkward with a stranger.

Despite the water concealing her body, Jennie covered her chest with her arms. She clutched her rag near her neck, pretending she was just washing there.

Tulsi dunked down, submerging her head. When she came back up - closer than before - she let out a big sigh.

"I'm glad to see you're safe." She settled in on a ledge near Jennie. "So tell me, who's Belle?"

Jennie squeezed her rag. She wasn't used to having conversations with people while naked. "She's my best friend back home."

"I'm sure you miss her."

"I do... and my family. I worry for them. I don't know if

it's more dangerous inside the wall with the corruption or outside with the lemerons."

Tulsi breathed out heavily through her nose. "I'll take corruption over lemerons any day. When you're nearly killed by one, it really puts things into perspective."

"You're right. One nearly got me on our way to Arborville. If Ethan hadn't... well, he saved me."

"One did get to me today. It grabbed my ankle and was pulling me off the platform..."

Jennie squeezed her rag even tighter, water trickled down her arms. "It didn't bite you, did it?"

"No. Someone shot it through the eye with an arrow before it could. Whoever that was, they saved my life."

Jennie relaxed her grip on the rag, lowering her arms. The light was too dim to see anything beneath the water, anyway. "It was Ethan, he told me, he shot a lemeron to save you."

Water sloshed around as Tulsi scrubbed her own skin. "Leave it to Ethan to save the day."

"He's pretty good at that," Jennie agreed. "Did you know he and his father were fighting them on the ground?"

"Foolish Ethan has a death wish."

"No, I don't think so. He did it to save Arborville and us. I wish he wouldn't do things like that, though. I don't know what I'd do without him."

"Me neither."

A thought occurred to Jennie. Why hadn't she realized this before? Tulsi and Ethan grew up together. They were close. She was the first person he went to when he couldn't stay in his own home.

"Do you have feelings for Ethan?"

Tulsi laughed. "Don't worry, Jennie, he's not my type. Besides, he's like a little brother to me."

Jennie sighed and scrubbed her knee. "Speaking of family, it seems like Ethan and his father are back on good terms. I guess facing death together will do that."

Tulsi hit the water with a crack. "I hate these damn monsters. Today's was the worst attack I've ever seen. Their numbers are increasing. Where does it go from here? They attack again tomorrow, and this time they actually do get into Arborville?"

"They're collecting at the wall surrounding my settlement. I don't even want to think of how many are there now. If we destroy those lemerons, others shouldn't be drawn through Arborville. But there's still the docile issue…"

"What's a docile?"

Jennie blinked, dazed. "You don't have them here?"

"How can I answer that question, since I don't even know what a docile is?"

"Right… I guess I just thought you might have them too. A docile is like a lemeron, except it doesn't have the same urge to kill. They do simple tasks around the Commune, but only from within an enclosed cell. We have this special blue glass to keep them contained and passive. It turns out, lemerons are drawn to dociles just like they are to each other. Things turned bad when we found out this secret group called the Order was abducting our people and turning them into dociles."

"So the dociles are why we are dealing with the sudden influx of lemerons? You and your people are the reason we were almost annihilated?" Tulsi snapped.

"Wait, are you accusing me of having something to do with this?"

Tulsi narrowed her eyes. "Maybe. What you say next will help make up my mind."

"I've been trying to stop the people responsible," Jennie said defensively. "I never knew they could be created, but this group is using the process to take out anyone who stands against them."

"That's the corruption you mentioned earlier?" Tulsi asked.

Jennie blushed, embarrassed of the wretchedness taking place in her community. She doubted anything like that happened here.

"Yes," she admitted.

Tulsi scoffed. "Well in that case, I'd like to change my earlier answer. I'll take a lemeron attack over that kind of corruption."

"If we don't do something about all the dociles in the Commune, it will only draw more lemerons."

"What are you going to do about it?"

Jennie wrung out the rag and scrubbed her face.

"I don't know. That's where I need Belle. She's better than me at figuring these things out."

"If we help get rid of the lemerons at the wall, that should give you time to fix things inside your community."

Jennie's heart fluttered with hope. "So, you're agreeing to help?"

"I'm only one person, but yes, I am. I'll try and get the others to help too."

Jennie's grin tugged at her scabbed lip, but she didn't care. She was finally on track to help save her people. She couldn't wait to tell Marlene.

THIRTY-FIVE

Marlene
———————————

Here she was again, resigned to a tower to look out the window at life happening below. Only it was a sleeping loft instead of her spacious chambers in the Sanctuary tower.

There was no privacy. There wasn't even room to stand. But at least she had a little porthole window to look through. She heard every word of Jennie's and Ethan's hushed conversation earlier. They were talking about her behavior during the battle. It should have bothered her, but she was numb.

Marlene shivered, freezing from inside. Shards of emotion flitted through her mind in tangled fragments. She tried to catch them, but they floated just out of reach, leaving her cold and haunted. She was losing herself to the curse.

Replaying the fight over and over in her mind, she tried to figure out what triggered her episode. The last thing she remembered was cutting down lemerons. Then it all went hazy. A fog blurred her vision. She remembered rage emanating through her body. It started from her chest, then spread all the way to her fingers and toes. Everything in her wanted to destroy, kill, devour.

It was the damn song. It got louder when she was

surrounded by lemerons. The closer she got to them, the louder the humming buzzed in her head. Now that the lemerons were dead, she was herself again... mostly. The song fading to a whisper in the back of her mind.

Looking out the window for an escape, she watched the aftermath of the battle. Men heaped the motionless lemerons and set them to the torch. The fire rose, licking the low-hanging branches, singeing the dying leaves. Why would they risk burning down their own homes to destroy a bunch of dead monsters?

Marlene frowned. That's exactly what she did before she left, only not in the literal sense. She upset the balance of everything when she addressed the Commune. She finally revealed Victor for what he was and told the people of the lemeron threat. She was pretty sure she called everyone a bunch of fools. They earned it, though, for letting Victor and his pet Sash bring this doom upon them. She figuratively burned the Commune to the ground and left her people behind to deal with the ashes.

It was time to tell Brenden about who she really was. He was her husband, after all. He deserved to know.

She climbed down the ladder and sat beside him.

"My love, there's something I need to tell you," she ran her finger over the red patch on his bandage. He would likely have a scar on his forehead, but he was alive.

"What happened to you today? You became someone else out there." He shook his head.

She sighed, her breath shaky as she exhaled. "No, not someone else. Something else. I don't really know how to tell you this, but I want no more secrets between us." Marlene began. "I have been alive for a very long time, over two hundred years."

Brenden frowned. "What? Is this some kind of joke?"

"No. I really am that old. It's possible because of my curse, as I like to call it."

"What are you talking about?" Brenden asked.

"It's best if you don't ask questions right now, maybe later. I'm having a hard enough time telling you this."

"Carry on then," he squeezed her hand.

"When I was in my thirties, I got sick. A lot of other people did, too. They called it 'Grey Fever' because anyone who got it had their skin turn grey. Their muscles would atrophy, leaving just skin draped over bones."

"That sounds familiar," Brenden cut in. "That's what the lemerons look like."

Marlene nodded. "I recovered from the Grey Fever, but I was the only one. Everyone else died, or so people thought. Before those who died were buried, they came back to life. But they weren't really living. There was no intelligence there, just anger, violence, and their intent to kill.

"The morgues and hospitals were the epicenter of it all. Grieving families gathered around their loved once who succumbed to the fever. As they mourned, those they lost woke up and slaughtered them all." Marlene shuddered. "You've never seen so much gore. I pray you never do."

Brenden's face grew pale and his hand twitched in hers.

"I watched as society crumbled. My father packed up our family and moved us to safety. But the disease spread. Soon people forgot the name of it. It didn't matter anymore, because there was no cure. Anyone with Grey Fever became known as a lemeron. It's derived from the Latin word 'lemures' which means 'ghosts.' That was when the world fell into ruin and became overrun with walking corpses." Marlene swallowed. "That was a little over two hundred years ago."

Brenden blinked at her. "No one, except for you, remembers how this all started. I can't believe you lived that long," he rubbed his eyes. "How is that even possible?"

"It turns out the lemerons can't die from old age, and neither can I. I'm cursed to live an eternity in a world consumed by destruction. I tried my best to carve out a safe place for my people. I founded the Commune two hundred years ago."

She squeezed Brenden's hand. "Only when I met you did I start living again. I was picking wild strawberries in the forest clearing when you approached. I was wary of strangers, but you showed me a kindness I hadn't experienced in decades. You shared your heart with me. You reminded me what it meant to have something to fight for."

Brenden placed a comforting hand on her arm.

"Today I saw you pinned down by lemerons. I had to destroy them for threatening your life. In doing so, my anger took over. I lost all of my senses except the urge to kill. It's an effect of Grey Fever. You hear the vibrations of the other lemerons. It's like a moth drawn to a flame. The more of them around, the louder the song, and the easier it is to succumb to it."

"Why are you telling me this?" Brenden asked.

"So that you understand that it wasn't really *me* who nearly killed you. It was the monster inside of me, my curse. It was the effects of Grey Fever taking hold of me once again."

Brenden shifted in his chair, taking her other hand in his. "Is there a way to help you get better?"

"Yes," she said. "Kill all the lemerons. Only then will I be free from the song."

THIRTY-SIX

Belle

─────────

B elle's first act as interim elder was to go to the wall. Travis and his father were among the twenty or so people accompanying her. Three people carried a very tall ladder. They wove through the apple orchard, the ladder catching on low branches.

Belle gagged from the stench. She covered her mouth and nose with her hands, trying not to throw up.

Mr. Caraway and Travis propped the ladder against the wall. It just reached the top.

"I'm going up," Belle announced.

Travis steadied the ladder as she climbed.

She had been up ladders countless times before at the solar farm, but never one this tall. It wobbled as her weight shifted from foot to foot on her ascent. The wood creaked under the strain of her weight. Her heart raced.

Don't look down, she told herself.

She grabbed a stone at the top of the wall. A piece crumbled from her touch and fell to the ground below. Pulling herself onto the ledge, she tried to catch her breath. With the stench wafting up from below, that was easier said than done.

She covered her nose with her sleeve, the fabric doing little to lessen the smell of decay.

Looking over the outer edge of the wall, she peered below. Her eyes grew wide at the sight.

"There are so many of them," she whispered.

It looked like there were a thousand gathered at the wall. They were in a constant state of motion. With no way forward, they still walked, bumping into each other and the wall. From above, their movements looked like ripples on the surface of water. Calm, but always moving.

Belle looked through the trees in the distance. More shambled her way.

"It's hopeless. There're too many," she said.

A snarl came in response.

One by one, the lemerons at the base of the wall looked up at her. Those yellow eyes gleamed with rage.

Her blood went cold.

All at once, they surged in her direction. They tore through each other, trying to reach her. Those closest to the wall took the most damage. Some collapsed to the ground, dead. More filled the gap, stepping on their dead kin.

A cold sweat broke out across Belle's forehead. She'd seen more than she wanted to. There were far too many to fight on the ground. If Jennie and Marlene brought back even a small army, the lemerons would overwhelm them. She had to do something. But what?

Climbing back down, she was relieved to be back on the ground. The stone wall would hold for a time, but it was crumbling.

Her thoughts drifted back to Jennie and Ethan. They left through one of the four gates. They were little more than wood doors that hadn't been repaired or reinforced in years. That had to change.

"What did you see up there?" someone asked.

The others looked on expectantly, waiting to hear her assessment.

"There are too many," she said.

"What are we going to do?"

Belle squared her shoulders. If she was an elder, interim or otherwise, she would do some good for her people.

"We've neglected our defenses for years. For far too long, we've assumed the wall would stand for hundreds of more years," Belle pointed to the stone that fell from the top of the wall. "But now it's crumbling, the gates are rotting. We will perish if we don't do something about it. Alan," she called out.

The man who helped Jennie's dad haul Victor away stood at attention.

"You and Mr. Caraway are blacksmiths. Forge braces for the doors."

"Yes, Miss Joiner," he said.

"Travis, work with Mr. Crow to replace all the rotten wood on the doors. Once you're done, help Alan and your father attach the braces."

"Okay, Belle."

"The rest of you," Belle put her hands on her hips. "We need scaffolding. Gather help from others and get to work. Build eight towers evenly spaced around the wall. We need to give our people a reliable way to get up there. Only then can we have patrols on the top of the wall. Our best bet is to defeat them from above."

"Where will we get all the wood?" Mr. Crow asked.

He was a middle-aged man and a skilled carpenter, just the right person to fix the doors. But he had a point. It would take a lot of wood to build the scaffolding. They couldn't risk sending anyone to the forest to chop down trees. She looked around the Commune, searching for the answer. Then it came to her. She smirked.

"We can use more than just wood for the scaffolding. I

know where we can get a lot of concrete blocks and blue glass... the strongest building material we have."

Mr. Crow crinkled his forehead.

"Where are we going to find all that?"

"Underground," Belle crossed her arms.

Time to level the playing field, Isaac.

Belle and her builders would tear apart the Order's secret processing facility, and there was nothing they could do to stop them.

THIRTY-SEVEN

Sash

For the first time in over a week, Sash travelled the dank tunnel beneath the Commune. The lab behind him, revenge in front of him.

He licked his lips. He couldn't wait to get his hands on that curly-haired girl again. She would pay for attacking him and escaping. No one ever got away from him. Sooner or later, he always tracked down his target.

It was more important than ever to take her out. He couldn't understand why the Commune people would elect *her* of all people. She was just a stupid girl. Now that she was an elder, she would have influence and power. Gnashing his teeth, he grumbled.

She was nothing more than a filthy undesirable. Belle Joiner had to go. Now that Isaac sanctioned her removal, Sash would make sure that happened. He already gave her a chance to become something greater than the filth she was. But she threw that away the moment she jabbed him with that needle.

Sash wouldn't even bother with processing her anymore. No. He would just wrap his hands around her skinny little neck and squeeze the life out of her. He clenched his fists, imagining the feeling of her throat crushing in his grasp.

He ascended the steps, emerging in the little shack concealing the tunnel entrance. Voices drifted through the cracks in the old door.

"This is the place?" A man asked.

His voice was familiar. Sash frowned, trying to place it.

"Yes. We'll find what we need in there," a girl answered.

This wasn't right. No one was supposed to know about this place except for those in the Order. These people were undesirables.

"Let's break it down," the man said.

Sash knew that voice. The memory of who owned it tugged at the back of his brain. He just had to think. He remembered hearing it when it was dark outside. Squeezing his eyes shut, he tried to remember.

That's it.

His eyes snapped open. That man was the scum who ran away. Sash remembered that night when he interrupted a meeting between two undesirables. He incapacitated and bagged the woman - Madam Marie as he found out later - but this coward ran. Sash vowed that eventually, he would get him. Today was the day.

"Perfect," he sneered.

He could take him by surprise. It didn't matter that he was with a girl. He would get his target first and get her after.

Sash flung the door open. Rushing forward into the daylight, he body-slammed the man, knocking him to the ground. Sash landed on top of him. He yanked the black bag from his back pocket. Pulling it over the man's head, he cinched it closed around his neck.

He was in his element. Everything around him faded away, leaving only Sash and his victim.

The man held up his arms defensively and tried to pull the sack off his face. Sash went for the tranquilizer to stop his squirming. Sash uncapped the needle with his teeth and raised his arm, ready to plunge the needle into the man's neck.

Just as he was about to bare down, someone grabbed his wrist and wrenched the syringe out of his hand.

"What?" Confusion flooded Sash's mind.

Awareness of his surroundings returned to him. He pulled his attention from the victim he pinned to the ground. All around him were feet and legs. He lifted his gaze and froze.

At least two dozen people surrounded him, all with various states of shock and anger on their faces. Many of them were shouting their disgust at him. They carried with them hammers, axes, and other work tools. All of which could be used as weapons. Did they coordinate this? Were they planning to kill him?

Sash climbed off the man, backing away from the mob. The curly-haired girl, Belle, stood directly in front of him. She folded her arms across her chest and gave him a look that said, "gotcha."

THIRTY-EIGHT

Travis
———————

Travis grinned. Sash, the untouchable terror of the town, was caught red-handed. There was no Victor to protect him now, either. Isaac could try, but with so many witnesses, what could he do?

Alan ripped the black sack off his head. The others closed in around Sash, blocking his retreat into the tunnel. His father looped a rope around Sash, pulling it tight. He struggled, but his arms were pinned. There was nothing he could do.

Alan kicked Sash's legs out from under him. His body slammed to the ground with a loud thud. His face flushed red with anger.

"What are you doing? Let me go," he ordered.

Jack tied his wrists together with impressive speed.

"That's enough out of you," Alan grunted, rubbing the back of his head.

Belle stepped forward. "Lock him up in one of the empty docile cells in the kitchens. Keep two guards on him at all times."

Two men hauled off Sash in the direction they came.

"Serves him right." Travis said.

"Now, with that ugly business out of the way, let's get to work," Belle stepped through the door to the shed.

Travis and the others followed.

"This is the first thing to go," she gestured around her. "The wood is old, but solid. We can use it. You five start dismantling this shack. The rest of you, with me."

"What is this place?" Alan asked.

"A facade, Mr. Thompson," Belle answered.

"For what?"

"You'll see," Belle pressed forward into the darkness.

Travis remembered there were steps at the back. He lit his lantern. Shadows sprung to life around them as the little flame danced. Catching up to Belle, he helped light her way.

Down they went. It was just as he remembered it. He swallowed.

Why did I agree to come here?

Belle kept her head held high, and her steps didn't waver. Drawing from her bravery, Travis picked up his pace. He had more help this time, and he knew what to expect - for the most part - at the end of the hall.

They came to the bend in the tunnel. Almost there.

But how would they get in? Last time he and Ethan got lucky.

Belle didn't pause to think when she reached the lab entrance. She just banged on the door until the little viewing window opened. The man with the funny goggles appeared in the opening.

"Alex, open up, it's Belle," she said.

Travis couldn't see his eyes, but he felt them. The weird man's face moved around as he scanned the group through his tinted lenses. Alex slid the little door of the viewing window shut.

They stood in silence. Nothing happened.

"Now what?" Travis whispered.

"We wait," Belle said

Travis shifted uncomfortably. This wasn't working out as he expected. They could chip away at the walls to break through, but that would take too long.

The door groaned as the rusty lock disengaged.

Travis raised his eyebrows, surprised when the door opened.

Belle stepped forward, Travis at her side. Having his father and everyone else gave him confidence. Together, they were stronger. And the Order's secrets would soon be exposed.

Alex stood in the middle of the room, wringing his hands nervously. When everyone entered, Belle turned around and addressed the group.

"Take that door off its hinges, and use it as a platform for the scaffolding."

Smart. Without a door, they can't seal this place off anymore.

"Take that door, too," she pointed at the opposite end of the room. "Rip everything apart. Salvage what you can and haul it out of here."

Travis's father set to work on the door with a crowbar. A few others joined in. Working together, they popped the door right off its hinges.

"How do you know about this place?" Alan looked around the room. His eyes settled on the morgue drawers.

"I was held prisoner here," she crossed her arms and nodded at one of the tables in the room. "Sash tortured me right over there."

The machines were still in place. Travis remembered Jennie hooked up to one when he came here with Ethan. He could still hear her screams from the electrical current running through her. Thankfully, it looked like no one got around to repairing the wires after Ethan cut them to free Jennie. It was still broken.

Alan went to the equipment. His face twitched as he

shook his head. He smashed the machines with his hammer, sending pieces flying.

"Take the tables out of here," Belle said. "We can use them for building. Salvage everything."

The room was a flurry of activity.

"Not my machines," Alex protested, gripping at his cheeks. "No, put that back. Stop tearing my cabinets off the wall."

He spun around, pulled in every direction, trying to stop everyone from destroying his lab. He tugged at his short messy hair, sinking to his knees.

"Why?" he cried out.

"Because together we need to save the Commune," Belle said. "Aren't you tired of just being a jailor? Don't you want to be a valued scientist again?"

She walked past him, letting him consider her words. She entered his office and stacked up the remainder of his files. She took a lot of documents the last time they were here, but now she collected the rest.

"Travis, Mr. Caraway," she beckoned to them through the glass partition. "We need to get all these documents somewhere safe. Don't tell anyone where you're taking them in case we have someone in the Order here with us."

His father nodded. "I know where to take them. Come on, let's get this done."

They bundled up the files with some of their rope. It didn't do a good job of concealing what they were hauling, but they didn't have anything else.

Alan finally got the other massive door off its hinges. He stepped through the opening.

"Jumping juniper," he exclaimed.

He re-entered the lab, his eyes wide. "There's an entire crew of dociles down here. Did anyone know about this?"

Belle left the office to address Alan. "Yes. Victor, Sash,

Isaac, the rest of the Order, Alex, and their victims," she stated flatly.

"Isaac? I don't understand. Is he a victim or with the Order? Did you know about this? You kept mentioning the blue glass, so you had to. How?"

"Isaac's goals are not aligned with ours. He's with the Order. Sash brought me here and tortured me. I was next in line to be turned into a docile."

Alan's jaw fell open. "You've got to be kidding. First Elder Victor's with the Order, now Elder *Isaac*? How did you get out? This place is built solid."

"It's a long story," Belle turned and addressed the others working on removing building materials. "Start working in there. Break apart those cells and haul the building materials to the wall. We need it all for the scaffolds."

"Come on," Travis's father whispered to him. "Let's go while everyone's occupied."

They slipped out of the office, heading for the exit.

"What do we do with all the dociles?" Alan scratched his head. "If we tear out the glass, we don't have anywhere to hold them."

Travis glanced over his shoulder, curious about how Belle would answer. She looked off into the distance, her mind going somewhere else. After a moment, she refocused on Alan.

"Free them."

THIRTY-NINE

Belle

A lan gaped at her, aghast. "Surely you can't mean it. The enclosures keep us safe from any harm they might do to us."

Belle stood at the threshold of the docile corridor. The blue glass allegedly kept the dociles, docile. But these weren't dociles, they were victims.

Anger boiled within her chest. The last time she was here, the Order threw her in one of those cells like an animal. Her teacher was being held captive in the cell across from her. Victor told the entire Commune that a lemeron had attacked and killed Mrs. Townsend. That was a lie. Sash abducted her and brought her here.

Mrs. Townsend revealed herself to Belle and communicated with her. Not with words, but with gestures. There was intelligence still behind those eyes. The Order was out to suppress it.

Belle screwed up her face. At the time, Mrs. Townsend appeared to be undergoing a forced transition into a docile. What if the people behind the monstrous shell could be restored? What if she could save Mrs. Townsend?

She had to try. It all started here. The first step was to start treating them like humans again. They would figure out the rest later.

"Come with me," Belle ordered Alan.

Taking a deep breath, she stepped into the corridor that had once been her hell.

"I want you to look in each and every enclosure as we pass and tell me what you see." She kept her eyes straight ahead as she spoke.

"Dociles. But I don't understand why they're here or where they came from."

Giving Alan the opportunity to take it all in, they continued in silence. Finally, she stopped. She shot a quick glance to the left at the enclosure that once was hers. It remained empty. Did Alex plan to stick her back in that cell as soon as he got the chance?

Belle turned her back on it and approached the enclosure opposite it. She knocked on the glass.

Alan's eyes grew wide. "What are you doing? We're not supposed to engage with the dociles."

"According to who?" she asked.

"The elders," he stressed.

Belle's lips curled. "I'm an elder now, and I'm engaging."

Movement within the dark cell pulled Alan's gaze. A gaunt figure wearing a blue dress shuffled forward. The stiff fabric still held the shape of voluptuous curves, but the skin wrapped skeleton beneath did nothing to fill it out. Wisps of brittle hair clung stubbornly to the docile's grey scalp. A slight twitch in its face resembled a hairless eyebrow rising.

She still remembers me.

"Alan, this is my teacher, Mrs. Townsend."

He let out a long breath. "Marlene was right. Victor was turning us into dociles. Hearing about it is one thing, *seeing* it just knocks the sense right out of you."

"Release her, and all the others," Belle commanded.

He hesitated. "Won't they go crazy like the lemerons if they're all together? Pack instinct, and what not?"

The docile Mrs. Townsend slowly shook her head. Belle beamed at her.

"See? She says nothing to worry about. Besides, think of the bigger picture. They can help us build up our defenses and fight the lemerons."

"If you say so..." Alan said, his tone filled with doubt.

"Go get some others to help you open up these cells. Bring Alex, he'll need to unlock them first. Then salvage the building materials."

He nodded and went back to the lab, leaving Belle alone. A shiver ran down her spine. She was right back where she swore she'd never return. It was an improvement from the last time though, at least now she was on the right side of the glass.

Mrs. Townsend placed her palm on the blue glass. Belle lined up her hand, resting it against hers. The surface was cold to the touch, sending another shiver through her body.

"I'm going to get you out of here," Belle promised.

Someone shouted in the lab. Belle snapped her head around to see what was going on. Alan was dragging Alex to her by the arm. He was flailing his arms, protesting the whole way.

"It's not right," he shouted. "You're destroying everything. I won't let you take my beautiful creations away from me."

Disgusting. Belle scowled. *He's talking like these dociles are his trophies.*

Alex stilled when he saw her. "You, you did all this just to get back to your enclosure," he laughed in a high pitch squeal.

He's lost his mind.

"I'm not setting foot inside one of those prisons."

"Yes, let's start the process right away. You were always my favorite. I can't wait to deliver you to a higher purpose."

Belle slapped his cheek to stop his mad-scientist dribble. "The only thing you're delivering is your keys into Alan's hand."

Alex cocked his head to the side, his tinted goggles reflecting the blue sheen of the glass. "I don't understand. Why don't you want to become something greater?"

"Because I have a higher purpose for you," she said, using his own words. She stepped closer, squaring her shoulders. "You are going to reverse this process. Instead of creating more dociles, you'll return them to their previous human state."

He rubbed his cheek and mouth with a clumsy hand. He mumbled as he thought out loud. "R-reverse it? Never been done before. But it could be. Most recent subjects ideal candidates for control cases." He gasped and mumbled on. "What of the dociles that have always been? Need to know if I can reverse it in them, too. Yes. Yes, this - this is a stimulating challenge."

He refocused and addressed Belle directly. "I've thought it through," he said, excitement bubbling over. "I'll do it."

Belle smirked. "Good. Now hand over the keys."

Alex reached into his pocket and pulled out a large ring filled with keys. He dropped it in Alan's outstretched hands.

Belle nodded. "Let him go."

Alan released his grip on the scrawny scientist.

"Yes. Who to start with?" Alex mumbled while pacing. He stopped, a smile spreading across his face. "Of course. Victor is mid-transition. I can stop it and reverse it before the process is complete."

"Did you say Victor?" She asked.

"Yes. Yes. Victor."

Belle and Alan exchanged a questioning look.

"I thought he was locked up. How did he get down here?" Alan asked.

"Isaac brought him," Alex pointed further down the corridor. "He's just a few enclosures that way."

She swallowed. Of course, Isaac got access to Victor. Both men were dangerous, and part of the Order. Maybe this would clue Alan and the others into the fact that Isaac can't be trusted either.

If anyone in the Commune deserved to be a docile, it was Victor. They could justify letting him rot in his cell and finish the transformation. How satisfying it would be to see her enemy destroyed and turned into a docile.

If I order his processing continued, I'd be no better than Victor. I'm nothing like him.

As conflicted as she was, she made up her mind.

"Do what you must, Alex, but move this operation above ground. No more hiding in the dark. And whatever you do, keep Victor locked up."

FORTY

Marlene

———————————

The stench of burning death filled the air as the lemeron corpses smoldered. Evening was pressing down on Arborville. The glow emanating from the burn pile did little to comfort those around. It was tainted. Cursed light fueled by the bodies of cursed creatures.

More lemerons would come, trailing behind those they burned. She knew their destination: the Commune.

The song buzzing in her head kept getting stronger. It called her back to the wall. Too many lemerons were gathering there. Marlene gripped the railing outside of Brendon's house. She dug her fingernails into the dry wood.

She lost herself from the influence of a few lemerons. What would she do with the call of over a thousand when she returned to the wall? If she wasn't able to snap out of it like she did today, what harm would she do to those she cared about?

It was a reality she didn't want to face but feared she wouldn't have a choice. She had to fight the threat to her people and her home.

"Are you ready?" Brenden asked from behind her.

She released her grip on the railing, turning to face her husband. "Yes. Let's get this over with."

Brenden raised a horn to his lips, giving it three short blasts.

The city built among the treetops stirred to life. Doors opened, the inhabitants gathering along the suspension bridges and decks outside of their treehouses. Brenden gave the horn another three blasts.

Ethan came from around the back of Brenden's house, Jennie trailing behind him.

"What's going on?" Her son asked.

"It's time we ended these monsters once and for all," Marlene stated.

Jennie's eyebrows rose. "All of them?"

Marlene only pursed her lips in response.

"I mean, how many are there in the world?" Jennie asked, looking puzzled.

"We destroy those plaguing us and the magnet that brought them here."

Jennie furrowed her brow. "You can't mean the dociles."

Naive girl. "We will do what we must to safeguard ourselves."

"But -"

Brenden cut Jennie off before she could finish her protest. "Our audience is waiting. You can continue this argument in private."

Marlene eyed the people spread amongst the trees. This was a hardened group. Most, if not all of them, wore some kind of weapon on their person. Even the children who couldn't be in double digits yet. They were always ready.

What a contrast to her own people. They were sheltered by the wall and brainwashed by the Order. They were victims of their own complacency. But no more. The rude awakening at the wall would force them to act. If they didn't, the

Commune would be overrun by lemerons, and there would be nothing, and no one left.

The people of Arborville had the right idea. Face the threat, train for it, always be prepared, and you'll never be caught by surprise.

Marlene stepped up to the railing, ready to address them.

"People of Arborville. Many of you don't know me, but that doesn't matter. I am Marlene from the walled town: the Commune. I am also Brenden's wife and Ethan's mother," she gestured with a hand behind her. "We come from two of the last remaining settlements in the world. We need to help each other and fight back against the lemerons if we are to survive."

Her crowd looked unimpressed.

"Today's attack was not random. These lemerons were only passing through to reach the Commune, where hundreds more are gathering. Arborville just happened to get in the way. Their blood lust overpowered the call of their kin. Today we all survived," she swallowed, remembering how she almost killed Brenden. "Tomorrow, we might not be so lucky."

"What are you asking of us?" A man shouted from one of the higher treehouse balconies.

"Come with me to the Commune. Help us defeat the lemerons at the wall. Together we can destroy the threat that plagues us both."

The man shook his head. "You said you have a wall to protect you. We have our height to protect us. I see no point in leaving to fight your battle."

Marlene frowned. After today's attack, she thought they would see the need to fight back.

"Chester, did you miss how they learned to climb?" A girl spoke up from a few trees away. It was Ethan's friend, Tulsi. "Did you miss how they almost killed me? We can't hide in the trees anymore. Sooner or later, they will get us. After today, I'd say we're out of time." She fixed her brown eyes on Marlene. "I will fight with you, even if Chester won't."

Marlene nodded. The girl had spirit, that's for sure.

"And what of the rest of you?" Marlene shouted.

She scanned the trees, eyeing every Arborville resident gathered. Those that met her eyes were her fighters. They didn't need to speak up for her to know they supported her cause. Those who's gaze fell when her eyes landed upon them were the weak ones. Cowards like Chester. She stared him down longer than the others.

"I ask again, what of the rest of you? Will you stand with me and fight or stay here and die?"

"Are those really our only two options?" Ethan whispered beside her.

Clever boy. There was always a third option for those determined enough to find it. Regardless, it did not serve Marlene to explore other solutions to this problem. She needed fighters, and she needed them now.

She narrowed her eyes at Ethan. He pressed his lips together, stifling any other comments.

No one else spoke. Marlene's face twitched with anger. After enduring an unprecedented attack today, these people were shaken. Despite all their claims of braving the lemerons, they were still weak, just like those in the Commune. It was easier to deny the threat existed than to actually address it.

It was time to take action. If they wanted to stay here and die, so be it.

"We leave in three days. Those not coming with me, I wish you a good death."

She turned her back on the gathered crowd, looking down at her like birds perched in the trees. She brushed past Brenden and went into his house.

She collapsed in a chair and pinched her brow. The buzzing at the back of her mind was giving her a headache. It was a whisper, beckoning her to the darkness. She feared it would get so loud it would drown out her senses.

Brenden entered the house and sat down in the chair beside her.

Marlene stared into the cold logs on the fireplace. "Long ago, I witnessed the transformation."

"What transformation?" he asked.

"Back before I founded the Commune, I was part of a band of people. We were migrating north, fleeing the growing number of lemerons. Eric, our arrogant leader at the time, was bitten by one. It didn't take long for him to change. He became a lemeron. He attacked me, so I killed him."

"That must have been horrible," Brenden said.

"The worst part of it was his face. Unlike the rest of the lemerons with gaunt skulls covered in grey skin, he still resembled the man he had been. When I think back on it, I see Eric attack me. Not a lemeron. But his mind was consumed with their song. He was a monster. He's what I fear I'll become."

"Don't worry, they will fight with us," Brenden placed his hand on her shoulder.

She reached up, taking his hand in hers. "They agreed to fight?"

"No, but I know them. We don't sit idly by when threatened."

"We shall see," she said skeptically.

"It's been a long day; you should get some rest." Brenden kissed her forehead before climbing to the sleeping loft.

The burden of protecting her people weighed heavily upon her shoulders. It was made worse by the fear growing within her. When she was closer to the hoard of lemerons, could she fight the song?

Exhausted, Marlene closed her eyes.

She could see Eric etched inside her eyelids. He rushed at her, teeth bared. He was another victim of the Grey Fever infection, another lemeron. Reaching his arm back, he prepared to strike her. His skin melted away, revealing a mirror image of herself. Her lemeron doppelganger swung its clawed hand forward, slashing her neck open. She collapsed to the ground, clutching at her throat. Marlene's lifeblood drained from her.

When she looked up, a grey fleshed lemeron stood above her. The last of her humanity was dying, leaving behind just another monster. Marlene closed her eyes, giving in to the darkness. The song hummed louder than ever.

She gasped, snapping her eyes open. Her hands felt frantically at her neck. It was dry, there was no gash. She was sitting in the chair in Brenden's house. She was still herself and alive.

It was only a nightmare.

Or was it a glimpse of my future?

FORTY-ONE

Ethan

E than took Jennie to the main hall the next morning. His breakfast porridge tasted bland today. Old Nan always made it the same, but something was missing. Maybe it was his lack of faith in everything.

Jennie ate silently from her bowl. She kept looking around the crowded hall.

"Why do they keep staring at me?" she whispered to him.

Ethan's mouth twitched into a smile. "It means they are willing to fight. You're a walking, breathing human being. There aren't that many of us left. You're one of us."

"One of *you* here in Arborville or one of the humans?"

There were those butterflies in Ethan's stomach again.

How did I mean it? I love Jennie and never want us to be apart.

"Jennie, you're someone I could spend the rest of my life with, and I want to. But after all the fighting is done and things return to normal, what becomes of us? Will you want to live in the Commune?" he swallowed. "Or will you consider living in Arborville with me?"

Her eyebrows raised and her mouth went slack.

His porridge sloshed around in his stomach. How would she answer the question hanging in the air between them?

"Can you believe Chester?" Tulsi huffed, plopping down at their table.

Ethan bowed his head to hide his flushed cheeks. He poked at the lumps in his porridge with his spoon.

"Come on, Tulsi, you know he's a blockhead," he said into his bowl.

"He is not. He's just stubborn, like me. Really though, he should do a better job picking his battles. Arguing with your mother about not joining this fight is like throwing dry leaves on a fire expecting to put it out. It doesn't help."

Ethan studied her. Her cheeks were red. "It almost sounds like you're defending him, then insulting him. What's going on?"

She slammed her spoon down on the table. Jennie jumped beside him.

"It's like he doesn't even care that I almost died yesterday. I was almost *eaten alive* by those monsters. How am I supposed to feel about that? Chester was wrong to so openly dismiss this whole mess… and to dismiss me."

Her hand shook as she grabbed her spoon and shoved a bite of porridge in her mouth.

"Chester's a true fighter, but he's also a sentry. Maybe he feels like leaving Arborville would be abandoning his post."

"Now you're defending him? What about your girlfriend? You're going to let him just turn his back on her problems? Well, I'm not. I'm fighting. Anyone who doesn't join in is a coward in my book."

Her cheeks burned red. She stuffed another bite in her mouth.

"Is Chester really so stubborn he won't help?" Jennie asked.

"He's loyal and dedicated to his duty. He'll come around," Ethan said. "Fighting lemerons is a responsibility that belongs to us all."

"If he's so loyal, why did he act like he didn't care a lick about me? He used to be so sweet. He always brings me flowers on my birthday. Next time he tries, I'm going to throw them in his face since he doesn't care if I live or die."

Ethan was at a loss. He had no idea what to say to Tulsi to make her feel better.

"Are you and Chester dating?" Jennie asked.

Ethan blinked. What? Tulsi and Chester? His best friend and *Chester*? He was a little too short, a little too disheveled, a little too... just not right for Tulsi... wasn't he?

"No," Tulsi shoved another bite in her mouth. "Besides, he wouldn't know a good woman if she hit him in the face. I know. I've hit him before. It was while sparring, but still," she shrugged. "The point stands."

Ethan raised his eyebrows. "Wait, what? You like Chester?"

Tulsi threw her spoon in her bowl, causing porridge to splutter onto the table. "Well, not anymore! He's a 'block-head' just as you said. He only cares about himself. Now you, on the other hand, you care. You're the one who saved my life. Jennie told me. Thank you for that."

He flushed. "That's what friends are for."

"No, that's what real men are for. Jennie, you're lucky to have someone like Ethan looking after you. Avoid the Chesters of the world if you can."

She crossed her arms and shifted in her chair. Looking around the room, she screwed up her face. Raising her voice, she addressed the others eating.

"You hear that? You're a coward if you aren't willing to fight for our world. We share it with other humans, like Jennie. If we don't look out for each other, who are we really? Are we going to be like *Chester* and just stay put in our own little bubble? Well, guess what? That bubble burst yesterday when the lemerons figured out how to climb. We aren't safe until that group at Jennie's wall is dead. Make your choice and make it quickly. In three days, I'm heading out. I hope you have enough sense to join me."

Tulsi stormed from the room, leaving her breakfast half-eaten.

"Wow, she really likes Chester, doesn't she?" Jennie asked.

"If you say so."

The idea of it was so strange. Ethan shook his head, bewildered. Both a couple years his senior, Tulsi and Chester had always been there, like older siblings.

"You really didn't know? I thought Tulsi was your best friend?" Jennie asked.

"Chester's a skilled sentry who's always reserved and focused. Tulsi's fierce and all over the place. She doesn't even have a specific job. She does a little bit of everything depending on her mood: sheer the sheep, go hunting, or help Old Nan wash dishes. They couldn't be more incompatible, right?"

Jennie gave a coy smile. "You'd be surprised how compatible people with major differences can be."

Ethan rubbed his temples. Too many aspects of his life were changing all at once. He wanted to focus on the immediate problem: the lemerons. It was a problem that never went away, but it was now a critical issue.

"Hey, Ethan."

He looked up to see Chaz standing nearby. "Morning, Chaz. What's on your mind?"

"I was standing guard when you two arrived. I've never seen anyone from outside come here, other than you when you were a baby, Ethan. When you brought Jennie here, it just solidified it for me. There are more people survivin' out there. We have to fight together if we're going to live through this." Chaz rubbed his bald head. "I'll fight with you. I'll do my part to convince the other sentries to fight, too. Even Chester. Although, he won't be happy about how Tulsi smeared him like that." He shrugged. "He'll get over it."

"Thanks, Chaz. We need your support," Ethan said. "The more people we can get to fight, the better."

"Thank you, Chaz. Really. Thank you," Jennie added.

"I'll get to it then," he nodded, then made his way for the door.

Jennie hugged Ethan.

He wasn't expecting it, but wrapped his arms around her, enjoying her embrace. The smell of apples in her hair was fading. She still smelled sweet, though, like morning dew on the leaves.

"Thank you, Ethan. We can't do this without you." She pulled away. "I need to thank Tulsi, too."

Jennie still didn't know her way around. He didn't blame her. It could get confusing navigating all the twisting platforms and suspension bridges.

He stood up, taking her by the hand. "Let's go find her."

FORTY-TWO

Jennie

B efore they left, the main hall grew more active with conversation. Jennie hoped that was a good sign. She couldn't make out what everyone was saying, but she hoped it was people agreeing to fight with the Commune.

She held Ethan's hand as they walked across the suspended bridges and platforms of Arborville. With his strong hand in hers, she felt like she could do anything. Today was a new day, and they would recruit more people to their cause. Tulsi and Chaz were just the start.

"Ethan, hang on," someone called out.

They stopped, turning to see a woman approaching from a bridge to their left.

"Alice, how are you?"

Her red hair was bundled on top of her head, crowning her freckled face. The wrinkles framing her green eyes made her look about Jennie's father's age.

"Just fine, thanks to you and Brenden. I saw what you two did yesterday. You faced the lemerons on the ground to save us all."

Ethan pulled his lips into a thin line. Jennie could tell he didn't enjoy remembering what happened down there. It didn't help that everyone kept talking about it.

"Everyone here owes you. If you and your father say we need to fight the lemerons at this wall, we'll do it."

Jennie smiled. People were willing to help. Chester resisted yesterday, but he seemed to be an outlier.

"Alice, we need every single person we can get."

She nodded. "Then you have me at your side."

"Can you help recruit others?"

"You can count on it. Many are already willing to fight, they just need the word from you and your father. I'll spread the word. Arborville is with you."

"Thank you," he said as she rushed off back the way she came.

"That was encouraging," Jennie said. "Is she a good fighter like you?"

"Everyone in Arborville is good at fighting. It's something we grow up learning as second nature. Like eating and sleeping."

Her stomach fluttered. Ethan was a fierce protector. If his people were half as good as him, then the Commune had hope.

"I don't know how we can thank your people enough. Facing a lemeron is nothing to scoff at, but to face an army of them..." She blew out a puff of air. "Everyone's so brave."

Ethan laughed. "Everyone except for Chester, according to Tulsi."

"Does she really think he's a coward?"

"No. She over-exaggerates sometimes. Chester's as brave as the rest of us. He's just focused on his responsibilities. He has trouble deviating from them, even when exceptions need to be made."

They continued on through the labyrinth of bridges. As they approached the edges of the town, Jennie wondered if they'd ever find Tulsi.

"Up ahead, we have our sparring grounds. They are platforms built around trees that won't support houses. We use the trunks and branches for target practice."

"Kind of like where I found you hacking at the tree with the machete the other night?"

"Mmm, not quite. That one will be someone's house someday. Maybe it's best not to tell them I was taking my anger out on their tree trunk."

Jennie chuckled. She had no idea who's house that would be. Who would she even mention it to?

"I won't tell if you don't."

"There she is," Ethan pointed to a platform two trees over. "Just as I thought."

Tulsi was sitting with one leg dangling over the ledge, and the other tucked under her. She was hunched over, working on something.

When they got closer, Jennie got a better look at what she was doing.

On her left she had a pile of blunt arrow shafts. To her right were the same type of shafts with sharpened tips.

Tulsi worked vigorously with her knife, sharpening the wood to a point. Each time she finished, she put it on the finished pile and picked up a new one. She must have sharpened at least thirty arrows.

Without looking up from her work, she greeted them flatly. "Congrats, you found me. I hope my outburst left you all entertained."

"Actually, I think it helped," Jennie said. "That's why I wanted to come and thank you. I appreciate someone who speaks their mind."

"Yeah, that's me. Always ready to jump to snap conclusions and make a mess of things."

"No, Tulsi. It's true. People are joining the cause. They're agreeing to fight with us," Ethan said.

She stopped sharpening, mid-stroke. Looking up at them. "They are? Who?"

"Chaz, Alice, and some more they've been talking with," he counted off.

"And Chester?"

"Not yet," he admitted.

She went back to sharpening arrows. "Coward," she mumbled.

Jennie shifted uncomfortably. She wasn't sure how she could help this situation, so she changed the subject.

"That's a lot of arrows. Are they all for you?"

"No, they're for everyone. There's no time to make the amount we need with proper arrowheads." She held the one in her hand up. "These will pierce a lemeron's thin flesh just as well as a tipped arrow. It'll kill one just as well, too."

"Good thinking, Tulsi," Ethan said approvingly.

Jennie's heart stopped when she heard something move across the ground below them. "What's that? A deer?" She peered through the leaves, trying to spot a pair of antlers.

Tulsi leapt up, gathering the finished arrows. She put them in a wool-lined bucket to have them at the ready.

Low groaning swept through the air.

"That's no deer." Ethan pulled his dagger from its sheath. "I need to sound the horn."

"Go Ethan! I'll protect Jennie." Tulsi snatched a training bow from the platform as Ethan took off across the nearest bridge.

Jennie's hands shook, but not from fear. Something inside of her snapped. She didn't want to need protecting anymore. She was sick of these monsters. They all needed to die. She was sick of being afraid of them and being helpless around them.

No more.

Never again.

She didn't know how to shoot a bow, but she did see a pile

of stones on the platform. She bent down, easing her hands under a large one.

It was heavier than it looked, but she heaved it up. Cold seeped through her sweater as she held the stone against her body.

Making her way to the edge of the platform, she watched the lemeron stagger closer.

"Jennie, don't. Let me take care of it," Tulsi whispered, aiming an arrow at the approaching threat.

"No," she hissed. "This one's mine."

Tulsi nodded, lowering her bow.

Jennie flashed a quick smile before turning her attention back to the monster.

Crackling rose from the lemeron's throat as it shambled forward. It was nearly beneath them.

Jennie hoisted the large stone over her head. She timed her throw carefully. Killing this beast on her first try was her only option.

Ethan sounded the horn from a few platforms away. But now the lemeron might see them and become aggressive. It would turn into a harder target. She had to kill it now.

She inhaled and thrust the stone to the ground with all her strength. It smashed into the lemeron's head in a brown explosion. It happened so fast; the monster didn't have time to croak before it fell, dead.

Her heart pounded. She actually killed her first lemeron. She would take control of her fear and use it to power through the fight with these walking horrors.

"You're stronger than you look." Tulsi gaped at her. "Grown men struggle with stones that large."

Jennie chuckled. "I didn't spend half my life throwing hay bales around for nothing."

"I can see that. Maybe you can teach us a thing or two."

She brushed the dirt from the stone off her hands. "Thanks. Maybe you can teach me to shoot a bow."

"Any time, Jennie."

Another horn sounded from a platform to their left. Then another echoed from further off.

Jennie bit her lip. "Are they just now responding to Ethan's alarm?"

She heard a groan from the forest floor. Then another. Her breath caught in her throat.

"More are coming," Tulsi readied her bow.

Jennie stood by the stone pile, ready to grab one when the time was right. She scanned the trees below, trying to spot any other lemerons. She hoped there would only be one or two stragglers.

Footsteps thundered over the bridge behind her.

"They're coming," Ethan panted. "There's at least six more."

Jennie's stomach plummeted.

Through the trees, she saw them approaching. Their legs shuffled through the dead leaves on the ground. Crackling groans carried on the wind, sending a chill through her.

She glanced behind her at the pile of stones and hoped there were enough.

Tulsi groaned. "Ugh… not again."

FORTY-THREE

Ethan

_____

"We need to pick them off before they get too close." Ethan loosed an arrow. It cracked against a tree trunk. "Damn it. I can't get a clear shot from here."

"The last thing we need is another pile of bodies for them to crawl up." Tulsi released an arrow, striking one in the leg.

It paused, swinging its head from side to side, trying to understand what happened. Seeing nothing, it continued forward, unbothered by the shaft protruding from its thigh.

"Nice shot," Jennie said.

"Not good enough, it's still moving." Tulsi nocked another arrow.

The lemerons staggered forward, weaving their way through the trees. Someone shot a crossbow bolt from a nearby platform. It sunk into the ground, falling short.

Ethan clenched his jaw. Footfalls landed heavily on the bridge behind them. He turned around, surprised to see Chester.

"Aren't you supposed to be manning the south platform?" Ethan asked.

"Alice has it covered. I wanted to be here with you," Chester's eyes darted to Tulsi.

A smile flickered on her face before she narrowed her eyes sternly at him. "Are you trying to protect me or something?"

"Huh? No. Yes," he shook his head. "Look, I want to make sure nothing happens to you like yesterday."

She rolled her eyes and turned back towards the approaching threat. "Then hurry up and load your crossbow. You're no good to anyone standing there like a tree stump."

Tulsi let loose another arrow. It got tangled in some lower tree branches before it even got close to a lemeron.

She growled. "This is ridiculous. We can't let them get close because we don't want a repeat of yesterday, but we can't get off a good shot yet. Some plan, Ethan."

"Then we just have to wait. We can't waste arrows," he said.

Jennie hovered near the pile of stones. "Do you normally have problems like this when lemerons come through here?"

"No. We usually have one or two lemerons at a time." Ethan gripped his bow and readied an arrow.

The lemerons continued their approach, leaves and twigs crunching under their feet. Their low groans got louder as they neared.

"This is too much. Are we going to have lemerons come through Arborville every day now?" Tulsi asked.

Ethan swallowed. "It's a possibility as long as the hoard at the wall is there."

He finally had a clear shot. Drawing back his bowstring, he took aim at one's head and released. He hit it between the eyes, toppling it over lifelessly.

The lemeron with the arrow in its leg emerged from behind a tree. Chester shot it with his crossbow, finishing the job Tulsi started.

"Two down," Jennie said.

Tulsi sent an arrow directly into one's chest. "Make that three."

The others from the next platform over fired off arrows, taking down one more.

Jennie picked up one of the bulky stones and approached the edge of the platform. One of the monsters with a crooked leg limped near. "This one's mine," she declared.

"Have at it." Ethan gave her room to line up her throw.

As it stumbled closer, Jennie raised the stone and took aim. She grunted as she hurled it at the Lemeron, hitting it on the side of the face. The creature's head snapped to the side, leaving its neck bent at an odd angle. It groaned, flailing its arms before falling down. It lay in the leaves, twitching.

"Well done." Ethan released an arrow, sending it into the monster's heart. It went limp, finally dead. "For good measure," he winked.

The last lemeron screeched. It dashed through the trees, running circles around some, trying to locate its prey.

"Moving targets are always harder," Tulsi said, keeping an arrow trained on it. Someone from the neighboring platform fired a crossbow, but the bolt missed. "You have to remember to lead your target." She released the arrow. It sunk into the lemeron's shoulder. It spun in a circle while Tulsi drew back again on her bow. "Sometimes you have to immobilize your mark before you can get a clean shot." She let go of the bowstring. The arrow penetrated the center of the lemeron's chest, killing it.

Tulsi lowered her weapon, facing Jennie. "Take that as your first lesson in archery. I'll teach you how to properly grip a bow next time."

Ethan raised his eyebrows. "Tulsi Amden, archery instructor? When did that happen?"

She shrugged. "Today. Jennie's got promise, you know. She might look like a fresh sapling, but she has some serious muscles."

Jennie blushed.

Chester peered over the platform, surveying the ground.

"I count seven dead lemerons. Six from just now and one from earlier?"

"That's right," Tulsi said. "That first one was Jennie's handiwork."

"Wow," Chester exclaimed. "There's nothing recognizable left of its head. Wouldn't want to piss you off."

Tulsi narrowed her eyes. "She's not the only one you don't want to piss off."

Chester scratched his head, messing up his already shaggy hair.

Ethan chuckled and leaned against the tree in the middle of the platform. "Now, we wait for the all-clear."

Jennie came over beside him, and he took her hand. "I'm proud of you," he said. "You took down two lemerons by yourself."

"Only one. You helped finish off the other."

"You still took it down."

Two short blasts from the horn sounded through the trees.

Jennie tensed as she snapped her gaze to the forest. "Are there more coming?"

Tulsi put her bow away. "No. That's the all-clear."

Jennie's shoulders relaxed as she let out a sigh. "I'm glad it's over."

"For now," Tulsi brushed past Chester, giving him a side-long look before leaving the platform.

He screwed up his face. "Why is she so mad at me? I thought she'd be happy I fought with her today."

"She thinks you don't care that lemerons almost killed her yesterday. She'll only be happy if you help fight the hoard at the wall," Ethan said.

"I do care that she almost died! But how can I abandon my post here? I have a responsibility to Arborville."

"So do we all, but others are willing to fight with Jennie and her people. We'll save Arborville by destroying the lemerons at the wall. Only then will attacks like yesterday and today stop."

Chester fiddled with his crossbow, pretending to clean it with his sleeve. "I'll think about it."

Three short horn blasts echoed through the trees.

"What's that one mean?" Jennie asked.

"Another community gathering. Come on." Ethan took her by the hand and lead her across the bridge.

FORTY-FOUR

Marlene

Marlene scanned the residents of Aborville collected on the platforms and bridges. Many met her eye, giving her a curt nod. These were her soldiers.

During the lemeron attack today, she helped Brenden stand guard on a northeast platform. She could see Jennie, Ethan, and his friends fighting off the lemerons in the distance. They had a better position than her for picking the monsters off one by one.

When Jennie heaved a stone up and crushed one of the creatures, it stunned Marlene. The girl had fight in her.

After the attack was over, Brenden pulled her aside. "We can't continue to survive daily lemeron attacks."

Marlene agreed. "Then, we move up the plan."

"I'll make the announcement," he said.

Brenden brought her to the center of Arborville, where he blew the horn. When everyone gathered, he squared his shoulders and addressed his people.

"We suffered the worst lemeron attack in our known history yesterday. Today we had seven more of the beasts threaten our community." He made a fist. "Enough is enough. We can't survive daily lemeron attacks for long. It's time we made our move to destroy the larger threat." He glanced at Marlene. "We can't afford to wait, we leave for the Commune tomorrow."

Some nodded their heads in agreement.

A stocky man with disheveled hair, who Marlene recognized as Chester, spoke. "What about those who can't fight, like Old Nan? Are we supposed to leave them here to fend for themselves?"

Chester, Chester. Always one to protest, aren't you?

"Anyone who can fight needs to come with us. The rest take up residence in the caves." Brenden pointed to the nearby cliff. "The entrance is off the ground and the best defense for those who stay behind."

"What if lemerons climb up into Arborville? Then they can cross the bridge and reach the caves just as easy as any of us," Chester said.

"That isn't going to happen." Brenden held out his hands like the answer was obvious. "But, in the worst case, they can cut the ropes suspending the bridge. When the bridge falls, it cuts off the only way to get to the caves."

Chester rubbed his head. "But the ties are thick, and if those who stay aren't strong enough—"

"Dear boy," Old Nan cut him off. "I can cut a rope as easily as the food I prepare. I'm not completely helpless." She winked.

Brenden nodded at her. "Those remaining here, bring any essentials and provisions to the caves. We can afford for a few scouts to stay behind and stand guard, but please no more than ten people." He slammed his fist on the platform railing. "I can't stress enough that we need our most skilled fighters with us. This won't be an easy battle to win, but losing is *not* an option."

Chester swallowed and looked up at the autumn leaves above as if they held the answer. Tulsi watched him from a neighboring platform, her lips pursed. She didn't berate him like she did yesterday. Perhaps she was waiting to see what he would do.

Chester leveled his gaze on Marlene. She arched an eyebrow at him, prompting him to speak up.

He either needs to help or go hide in the caves already.

He cleared his throat. "I'll fight beside you and your people. Although, I worry what will become of my own who stay behind."

Marlene nodded her approval at him. "The caves sound like the safest place for them. They will be protected."

"Good man, Chester," Ethan said. "Thank you."

Brenden looked around, as if taking in his home for the last time. "Everyone coming with us, get your weapons ready. Tomorrow we leave."

Marlene took Brenden's hand in hers, squeezing it. She accomplished what she came here for: she found her husband and her son and recruited a small army with their help.

In the coming days, they would fight to save both Arborville and the Commune. The hoard at the wall tugged at her mind, their song begging her to join them. She would destroy the lemerons or draw her last breath trying.

Acknowledgments

There are many people who supported me throughout the process of writing and publishing this book, including my family, friends, and loyal readers. You inspire me to keep writing so I can share my stories with the world.

Thank you to Brass Rag Press for making sure this story is the best it can be. Thank you to the amazing Covers by Christian for creating this amazing cover.

A special thank you to my readers who chose to read this book. You have many books to choose from, and I'm honored you selected my story. I sincerely hope you enjoyed reading this book. Thank you!

About the Author

Valerie Puri is an author of Paranormal, Fantasy, and Young Adult.

As an author of both short stories and novels, she enjoys the flexibility of writing tales of any length. Her favorite aspect of writing is the ability to create something out of nothing. She loves building worlds readers can visualize and filling those worlds with complex characters and storylines. Valerie believes that the experiences we have in life are just stories waiting to be written.

In 2016, she published her debut novel, The Crimson Tree, a thrilling paranormal tale inspired by true events. The main source of inspiration for this story was a number of experiences her sister encountered in her home. She went on to publish The Dociles, book one of The Secret Archives Trilogy, her young adult dystopian series. Valerie's work can be found in anthologies such as Demonic Anthologies, Thrill of the Hunt, and Once Upon Academy. Readers can look forward to future novels and short stories with paranormal and urban fantasy aspects in the near future.

When she's not writing, she enjoys spending time with her family, traveling, or listening to audio books. She is a Florida transplant, but part of her will always call the Midwest home.

www.valeriepuri.com

Also by Valerie Puri

The Secret Archives Trilogy

The Dociles

The Lemerons

The Undesirables (Coming Soon)

Standalone Novels

The Crimson Tree

Short Stories

Spite and Pride

Anthologies

Once Upon Academy: Year 1

Thrill of the Hunt: Buried Alive

Thrill of the Hunt: Cabin Fever

Demonic Carnival

Scary Snippets: A Halloween Microfiction Anthology

We Know the Truth, Do You?

www.ingramcontent.com/pod-product-compliance
Lightning Source LLC
Chambersburg PA
CBHW072235170626
46813CB00003B/1237